Bride by Mail

Richard Puz

EAST 74TH STREET PRESS*WASHINGTON

Copyright © 2013 by Richard Puz

Cover design by Julie Puz-Wilson

Library of Congress Control Number: 2013939369
East 74th Street Press Washington

ISBN-10: 098527798X

ISBN: 9780985277987

First Edition; Print Version

ALSO BY RICHARD PUZ

NOVELS
(Print and E-Books)

Six Bulls — The Ohioans
The Carolinian
Avenge

SHORT STORIES
(E-BOOKS)

Abraham
Arkansas Storm & Captain Jonathan Buzzard
Beanblossom Creek & Stain
Canyon of Death
Danny Boy & Tennie
Roaring River
Runaway Slave
Smoke
Sourdough Wind Mine
Three Bells & Newtonia

Dedicated to the love of my life ~

*And to the restless pioneers who migrated westward
to carve out new lives, and helped create a nation.*

*Throughout the writing of the Six Bulls series, many
have generously shared family tales and incidents involving their
pioneering ancestors. I am most grateful and wish to thank some
including W. Young, S. Poor, M. Epps, R. Edwards,
V. Westfall, D. Erwin, and many others. Additionally, I would
like to recognize the family tales written by Victor S. Sparling
and Capitola E. Weddell.*

Letters

CHAPTER ONE

February 1888
New Philadelphia, Ohio

"Father, stop!"

"Damn it, Ev, you've passed your third decade in life. You're no longer a spring chicken, nor are you a feather-head loon! In the next few years, you'll be an old maid, both in fact and age. And then, who'll have you?"

"Oh, for heaven's sake, not you or anyone is going to rush me into marrying Will Williams, or any other man," Eva stormed.

"My God, daughter, you've known him forever, and he asked you to marry him months ago. It's time that you set a wedding date." Hitching up his pants over his growing paunch and snapping his suspenders for emphasis, Isaac Helms stared at his daughter in bewilderment. "Don't you want to marry and have a family before you shrivel up like a prune?"

At that moment, Eva Mae Helms was in no mood to discuss her suitor. Instead, she was red-faced with anger. This was one of many times that her father had confronted her, and it was always for the same reason, "her failure," as he stated it, to be a proper example for her younger sisters. His conclusion was based on simple arithmetic. At her age, she was neither married nor already carrying her second or third child.

Independent-minded, she was determined to seek the life she wanted, and she had the self-resiliency to hold her own when talking to him. She simply was not ready to marry, at least not Will. Even so, it was definitely becoming more of a battle.

"Ev, please, your mother and I aren't getting any younger, and we want all our girls looked after before we pass on. And it's time we stopped mollycoddling you."

"Father, you are as strong and ornery as a bull, and mom is doing well."

"May I remind you that your older sisters, Viola and Mary, are properly married? They have settled down, with four youngsters between them. Your job at the public library in town can't be so important that it'd interfere with you marrying Will."

"I'm happy for my sisters, but I see life differently, and it is my life. A big, wide world exists out there, and I want to be part of it. Have you read any of the recent accounts of explorers finding new civilizations? Lordy, it's happening all the time, and adventurous fellows and their families are carving out lives in the virgin territory on America's western frontier. I just read the other day that Washington Territory has trees so big that three men with arms stretched wide can't touch fingers."

"What in blue blazes does the size of a tree trunk have to do with you and Will getting married? These days, girl, I don't understand where your head is."

"I know," she replied, staring out the window. "Father dear, I want to accomplish something with my life, see new places, do things, hunt game, maybe fish the rivers for the big ones and . . ."

"You want to hunt and catch fish?" Isaac Helms stormed, running his fingers through his graying hair. Sarcastically, he continued, "Rubbish! I can just imagine you wading into a stream with your bloomers showing, and your skirts and bustle pinned up high and dry. Ha, wouldn't that be a sight. You're just procrastinating. First, it was David, then James, and now it's this fine lad. Next, I suppose that you'll be waiting for some knight on a white charger to come along, and sweep you . . ."

Angrily, she interrupted, "I'm not ready to marry any man. Why can't you try to understand what I'm saying? Why won't you consider my views, and the things I want to do with my life?"

"Poppycock!"

"Even here in New Philadelphia, things are changing, with the construction of the new county courthouse and men paving Dover Boulevard with stone blocks from the limestone quarry and . . ."

"Enough! Ev, you're way past schoolgirl daydreaming. You need to marry, and, by God, I'm tired of us arguing all the time. Remember your place, young lady, I still provide the roof over your head and food on the table. And, good heavens above, it's time you cleared your mind and came to grip with your future. Will's an upstanding fellow who has a fine job at the grain mill. You just wait and see, he's on his way to making something of himself. You could do a lot worse, and you know it."

"Father, you're always pushing me to do this or do that. Can't you see that I'm torn by this decision? Will's a good and decent man. I only know that it doesn't feel right to me."

"Doesn't feel right?" he stormed. "By all that's holy, I'm trying to advise you about all the rest of your days, and here you are, mumbling about your sappy feelings. We both know that the Civil War left the country with a generation short of men, and other gents have gone off seeking gold in the West or got themselves lost in the wilderness. Ev, why not take what's in your lap and already offered."

"I won't be pushed by your nagging. And I'm tired of your constant bullying. It seems like every time we talk, you badger me about marrying Will."

"Girl, you still live in my house and I don't . . ."

"Well, I can fix that easy enough."

"Eva, go to your room."

"How dare you treat me like I'm a knee-high, sap-suckling youngster? I'm leaving, but it's to get ready for work." She whisked through the hallway arch, long skirts flying, only to turn and stop, a high flush on her face. "If you'd open some of the new books at the library or read the big-city newspapers, it would expand your mind beyond your stuffy cabinet shop, and you'd know what's going on in the world. Things are changing, and I want to be part of it!"

Shaking his pointed finger, Isaac Helms stormed, "Eva Mae!"

CHAPTER TWO

The Tuscarawas River flowed through tree-covered hills and bordered New Philadelphia on three sides. The city, founded in the eighteenth century, served as the center for mining and manufacturing operations in the region and was the county seat. The Helms house stood on Broadway, one of two main streets, and it was an easy walk to the center of the thriving community.

Even for February, the weather was very cold, yet everyone, including the *Farmer's Almanac,* predicted the likelihood of an early spring. In defiance of the bitter winter, the roses outside Eva's bedroom window showed new beginnings of reddish-colored stems.

She stood in front of the tall mirror, pinning up her hair up in a fashionable bun, and brushed the lint from her dark-blue dress. The upper waistcoat was close-fitting, which was the style of the day, topped by a white-fringed capelet. Below the waist hung a multi-layered skirt of the same blue color, which was draped over several stiffened petticoats.

Buried below, she wore her three-piece, strapped-on hip pad, which served as a modest-sized bustle, a style that had returned in recent years. She loved bright colors, yet restrained herself when dressing for work.

Examining the reflection closely, her auburn hair framed brown eyes, high cheekbones, and a light complexion. She knew that she was not a classic beauty, but her figure was trim, and she stood more than five feet tall in her stocking feet. *Yes,* she thought, *my features are passable, although Thelma up the street is more eye-catching.* Thinking about the redhead, she chuckled. *Yes, she certainly is an eyeful, walking down the street wearing her outsized, cage bustle, which sways her backside in rather heroic proportions. I've seen more than one fellow stop and look, as she walks down the street.*

Me, I'm average, she concluded. *Yet, there have been men attracted to me from time to time, like the banker across town and the apprentice working with father. And, of course, there's Will. Well, I am what I am. It's what I do with my life that's important.*

Recalling her father's tongue-lashing, tears welled in her eyes. *Oh, Dad, if you only knew what's tormenting me. Will's an agreeable fellow and cleaver enough, but I yearn for the strength of a man who is bold, fearless, and takes charge of his life; not one who is too timid and unwilling to make waves, like Will. Perhaps it'll be someone like Frank Sommer. Whoever the man is, I'm determined that it's going to be my choice, because it's my life.*

Hearing footsteps in the hall, she quickly wiped her eyes with a handkerchief. Soft knocks on the door preceded its opening.

"Ev, may I come in?" her older sister, Viola, asked. She wore a worried expression on her face. "Are you all right after that tirade?"

"Yes, and please close the door."

"You've been crying, and your eyes are red. I didn't mean to eavesdrop, but actually, everyone in the house heard his ranting. It's a wonder that the neighbors haven't complained. How are you holding up?"

"I'll be all right," Eva replied, as she picked up a brush and finished arranging her hair. "No one is going to push me into marrying any man. It's my future, and I'll live it as I choose, not what's customary or expected, nor birthing one youngster after another—until I'm rung out before my time." At once, she saw the pained expression on her sister's face, who recently had shared with her the wish to have another baby. Realizing how hurtful her words were, she said in a rush, "Oh, Viola, I'm so sorry. I didn't mean you or Mary. It's just that I'm unsettled in my thoughts and father has me riled up."

"I don't take offence, and you know that I love you. After your talk with him, I'm surprised that you're not more upset. Nevertheless, it's been four months since Will asked you to marry him. Why don't you make up your mind, one way or the other, and get beyond this point in your life?"

"I guess I should, yet I can't stop thinking about the Far West and places like Oregon and Washington Territory. Why, do you know that they have forests full of huge trees, where three men with outstretched arms . . ."

Interrupting, Viola asked, "You're really talking about Frank Sommer, that wild man in Washington Territory, aren't you?"

"I suppose you're right," she responded, blushing. "You've always been able to read my thoughts."

Viola was older by two years, about the same height, and her complexion took after their father, with light sandy hair and gray eyes. She usually dressed in gingham and wouldn't dream of owning a bustle, much less wearing one. A confessed homebody, her sister loved being a mother and wife, caring for her family in the small house located a block away.

On the contrary, Eva was more daring and showed streaks of stubbornness early in life. When she was barely eighteen, she applied for a job at the town library, a workplace where men held all the existing positions. After persistent efforts, she was hired. Over a period of years, she worked her way toward greater responsibility, and she had been appointed to the position of presiding over the library's purchase of new books.

The previous decade, however, did not fully tame her adventurous nature. She still easily lost herself in the accounts of explorers, such as David Livingstone, who wrote about the mysterious African Continent, or the latest Victorian sensation novels by Mary Elizabeth Braddon, the "queen" of circulating libraries, or George Du Maurier's diabolical Svengali in *Trilby*. While she found reading exciting, books provided scant release for her restless, inner spirit.

Eva had always enjoyed the attention of men, including Will. Before him, there had been others, yet none of the relationships lasted. Years earlier, she recalled strolling in the woods one Sunday, holding hands with a young man who lived across town. He was handsomely captivating and constantly in her thoughts. Suddenly, he drew her behind a tree and awkwardly kissed her on the mouth. It was more of a peck than anything else. She returned his kiss, pushing against him in a deeper embrace and, like a Braddon heroine, she slipped her tongue between his lips. Astonished, the young man broke apart, shocked and deeply embarrassed. To this day, he still blushed whenever they occasionally passed on the street.

There were other disappointments, too, and not just with the men recited by her father. Those experiences remained with her when men confronted her in the book stacks at the back of the library. The last time, the married man was more demanding, and his hands roamed freely, until her knee met his privates. Apparently, the word got around, as dalliances in the stacks no longer occurred.

With Will, things were different, and she was at ease with him. Yes, they kissed, but it was very proper and Victorian-like. He was about her age, handsome, and respectful. Hard working and ambitious, he was considerate and deferential to her. As a husband, she believed he would be a steady provider.

She readily agreed that all were laudable traits, and yet, in a strange way, these were also a source of vexation for her. *Take our discussion last Christmas, for example,* she recalled. *I thought it would be romantic if we eloped and took the train to Niagara Falls. I know the suggestion was a bit daring, at least for those of us living in New Philadelphia. Still, it sounded like adventurous fun. Ever the traditionalist, Will quickly went onto something else. Yes, he's predictable and, at times, a little boring.*

"Sister, dearest, come out of your reverie and talk to me," Viola said, giggling.

"Sorry, I was thinking about Will for a moment."

It was easy for the two sisters to talk, and they had shared many secretes over the years. Despite their different personalities and interests, Eva felt comforted by her sister's understanding nature and soft voice. She was the one person in the family who made no demands as a condition to her love.

"You can dream about Will any old time. I want to hear more about the wild man, Frank Sommer. I'll wager you recently received another letter from him."

"Yes, one arrived earlier this week."

"Well, what's the latest from the deep, dark woods? Don't just sit there with that silly smirk on your face, young sister. Tell me what the wild man from Washington

Territory has to say. Or, better yet, read one of Frank's letters to me."

Smiling, Eva reached under her bed and retrieved a beautifully worked, wooden box in which she kept Frank's letters. Briefly, she ran her hands over the polished finish before opening the lid. Many years earlier, it had been a birthday present from her father. Unlocking the lid, she shuffled through the contents and selected a brownish envelope.

"What news does he have this time?" Viola asked, cheerfully. "Did he write more about his adventures traveling west? Has he sent you a daguerreotype picture yet? Do he and his brother resemble each other?"

"No, Frank tells me that his brother is three years older, and that he was the tallest in the family, with fair skin and light sandy hair. And, no, he's sent me no image. I only know what I've already told you, that he's forty-eight, and his beard and hair are dark, while his eyes are blue."

"Hmm."

"Don't 'hmm' me. He's a mature man who knows hard work, felling giant trees, and panning for gold."

"Does he find much gold?"

"He says there's more than enough for his needs. I believe he's a modest man with fine qualities. Here, I want to read his words to you."

"January 10, 1888"

"January 10th," Viola interrupted, "and what is today's date? February 12, I think. My, the delivery of mail these days is unbelievably quick, isn't it? I remember father saying that letters could take three or four months, maybe longer, when grandfather used to write to our relatives back east."

"Yes, it's amazing. The railroads have provided a great boon for mail delivery. Sometimes with Frank, I almost feel like I'm carrying on a conversation with him. I know it sounds silly, but the speed these days is a real wonder. Of course, on his end, he paddles the nearly twenty miles downriver to Cadyville to receive and post his letters, and that adds days to our exchanges. Now, can you please hold your babbling for a few minutes, so we can get through this?" Seeing a grudging nod, she continued reading.

"Dear Eva,

Despite long bouts of rain, I've now fully cleared the land where I am going to build a new cabin. It will be sizable, measuring forty feet by twenty-five at the base. Over the past two years, I have cut the timber, and it has aged well. I am really looking forward to setting the first course of logs and getting it completed by the end of summer.

Your letters have made the long winter pass more quickly, and I thank you for that. I am overjoyed when I find one waiting for me at the village mercantile. Do you think that we will ever meet? I am sure it will happen, and when we do, it will be like a bright, sunny day after a spring rain for me, much the same as watching a beautiful rainbow stretched across a valley, pillared by the peaks of our tall mountains."

"My-oh-my," Viola commented, smiling mischievously, "he's a romantic soul, isn't he, this wild man of yours? Read some more, sister dear."

Blushing, Eva asked, "Do you remember that he and his brother ran away from their farm in Missouri when he was young?"

"Yes, and they traveled to Independence, and found jobs as outriders for a wagon train bound for Oregon. Why did they leave the farm?"

"He says that going west had always been their dream."

"By golly, what exciting times they must have had."

"You're right. Frank had just turned seventeen when they left, and Jonah, his brother, was twenty. They were into their fourth week of travel and were south of the Platt River, when the wagon train ran into trouble. Here's how he tells it."

"You asked about our adventures traveling west. We surely had a passel. One stands out, when we were confronted by the biggest doggone buffalo herd that I have ever run across. I watched the whole thing, yet it was an incident that still staggers my mind. I relay it, with the hope that you will not think of me as a man who stretches a yarn beyond its bounds, because every word is true.

Our wagons were strung out traveling through a broad valley, and Jonah and I were herding the cattle and remuda at the rear. It was one of those hot, humid days, when your clothes stick to you. We each wore a bandana over our nose and mouth to breathe easier, given all the dust thrown up by the wagons and stock.

Unexpectedly, we heard a gunshot, which came from the front of the column. Well, that captured our attention, as it was the signal for all the train's outriders to gather, and I mean pronto. We slapped our hats against our horses' haunches and galloped down the long line of wagons toward Ernie Fudge, the captain of our train. He sat his horse, staring westward and . . ."

CHAPTER THREE

Spring 1855
Nebraska Territory

Even from a distance, Captain Fudge saw that the wagon train's scout was riding at a breakneck pace, urging his horse recklessly down the steep hills that bounded the long valley. *Any report he's bringing can't be anything except trouble*, he figured. Raising one arm with his fist clenched, he signaled the train. Immediately, the sign to halt was passed down the line of covered wagons.

He spurred his horse, closing the distance to his hard-riding scout. With one hand holding the reins, he groped behind him with the other to retrieve his field glass from the saddlebag. Finally, he pulled back on the horse's reins and came to a prancing stop. For a better view, he wound the reins around the saddle horn and stood tall in the stirrups, focusing the telescope on the fast-approaching rider.

Shep, his right-hand man on the journey to Oregon Territory, was galloping as though the demons of hell were chasing him down the steep slopes, as he and his horse slid to the base of the hills.

Looking back toward the wagons, Captain Fudge pulled his muzzle-loaded pistol from the holster and fired it into the air. It was a signal to the settlers that danger was afoot, and the shot would bring his crew of lieutenants and outriders to him. As Shep neared, he noticed the man's wind-whipped look. The scout's horse was white with lather, and foam-flecks had blown back to the man's chaps, forming long streaks.

In a cloud of dust, Shep brought his horse up short and shouted, "Captain, buffalo stampede." Pausing to catch his breath, he continued, "They may be headed our way."

Captain Fudge couldn't hide his surprise. He expected to hear that there were more signs of Indians ahead, which was bad enough. However, a buffalo stampede could be even more dangerous.

"How big is the herd?"

"Can't rightly say," the scout replied, breathing heavily. "Their dust cloud stretches clear to the western horizon."

Puzzled, Fudge asked, "What do you mean, 'maybe headed our way?'" Nothing stopped a large stampeding bison herd, short of their becoming winded or toppling over a cliff, one after another, with their follow-the-leader instinct.

Still panting, the scout replied, "Ahead, the valley joins another fork some miles west of here. I didn't wait to see which way they'd go, deciding that I'd better warn the train."

"Any idea how it started? Are Indians hunting and running them?"

"Not that I saw."

"Well, something set them a running."

"Uh-huh, but it could be a pack of wolves hunting them, or something else."

At that moment, his two-dozen men arrived. Most looked around or stared westward, as the air was thick with questions. Yet, there were no unusual signs, or any visible danger on the horizon.

Shep asked, "What do we do, Captain? We've got the same chance of them coming this way, as we have of them taking the other fork."

"How long do we have?"

"Let me think," Shep replied, rubbing his dark beard and looking back at the hills. "I was on a high peak when I first saw them, and I returned the shortest way, along the ridgeline. The last I saw them, the herd was rounding some hills to the west and funneling this way. They have farther to travel because this valley follows the river, and both meander in a lazy manner." Removing his hat, the man ran his hand through his hair, which was plastered down with sweat. "Maybe twenty minutes, more or less."

The grizzled leader stared hard at his scout, saying nothing, but pulled out his pocket watch and noted the time. Looking westward, he quickly made a decision and motioned for his men to gather around, as he stepped down from his horse. Some of the men started to dismount until he shouted, "Damnation, stay on your ponies! We need every tick of the clock to survive the danger coming our way. Now, calm down and listen up."

Kneeling, he grabbed a stick and began drawing lines in the dirt, as his riders gathered around, some standing in their stirrups to see his scratches. "Men, nothing is more dangerous than stampeding buffalo, and there's a big herd headed our way. It may change direction, but we have to prepare for the worst. When these critters have fear in their thick, wooly heads, they become a brown tide of crazed beasts, and nothing can stop them, short of God striking them down. We have to be prepared and try to see it through without losing the whole train, and if they're coming our way, they'll be here about half past the hour."

The somber hush was broken only by nervous horses pawing the dirt, the rustling of tack, and leather creaking, as riders shifted anxiously in their saddles.

"Here is my plan," Captain Fudge continued. "We have more than one hundred wagons in the train." Catching the eye of a seasoned man in his crew, he ordered, "Medberry, you and Lyle take half the men and get the wagons lined up in four rows of about twenty-five each, all headed this way." Pointing, he continued, "George, Marv, and Clay, you go with them. Don't let anything get in your way. Understand, Medberry?"

"Right, Captain."

He pointed to four straight lines drawn in the dirt. "I ain't the greatest picture maker, but I'm thinking this'll give you the idea. Leave an open space between the double lines of wagons, wide enough for teams in harness to move through."

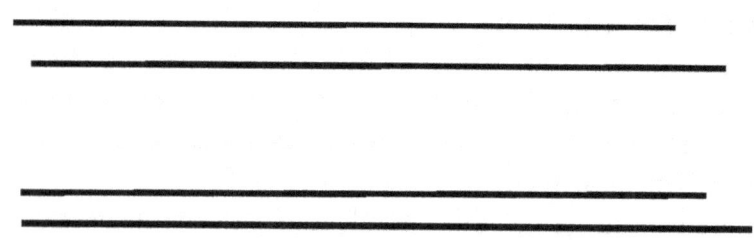

"Time is our enemy, and you got to be quick, so no dilly-dallying! Understand?" Not waiting for a reply, he hurriedly continued, "Then, see to it that ropes run from the lead draft animals to the axle of the wagon in front, not to tailgates, as excited teams are likely to rip them off when they panic.

"Shep, you, Smith, and Carlson, with the rest of our men, lead the last dozen wagons in front of the rows. I want them positioned to form the tip of an arrow, with the draft animals facing towards the rear." He continued, drawing small separate lines in the dirt to complete the chevron. "And overlap them. They'll become the point of the arrowhead that may divide the stampede and cause them to pass on the outside of the train. Unhitch the teams only from those front wagons and drive them into the middle, between the columns. Understand?"

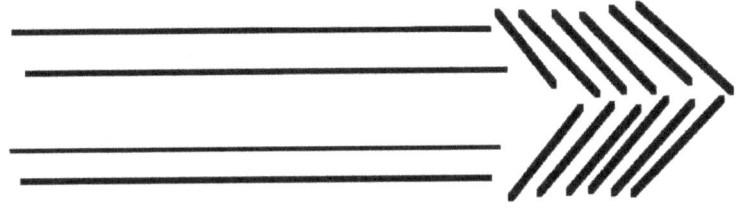

Shep nodded.

Fudge's voice was raw with emotion, conveying the urgency of the approaching danger. "Get the folks moving fast! Now hear me good—no stragglers! Use your bullwhips, or any other means, but get it done in the next fifteen minutes. And don't stop and explain to nobody, just say that danger is acoming."

Looking over his men, he spotted Jonah Sommer and his younger brother, Frank. "You Sommer boys grab anyone else on horseback and drive all the extra stock and remuda at the rear of the train over the hills that border this valley to the north, and keep them there until you hear different. Oxen fear buffalo more than death, and they'll bolt at the first whiff. They may be slow and sluggish, but once they get the scent, it'll scare them out of their wits, and halting them is going to be like us trying to stop the hairy buffalo herd headed our way."

One of his riders started to turn his horse away to follow orders.

"Dadblast it," Captain Fudge shouted. "Where in the hell are you going, you knucklehead? I ain't finished yet." Waiting impatiently until he had everyone's attention again, he hurriedly continued. "When the line of wagons and arrowhead are formed, you tell the men to stay in the rigs with their brakes fixed, so they can try to control the animals from joining the stampede. Believe me, they'll have their hands full. Everyone else that's at least hip-high is to come forward with their guns and form up behind the lead wagons."

"But, Captain," Shep said, "the men are much better shooters."

"Don't make a damn hill-of-beans difference," the leader snarled. "When we start shooting, no one will have to aim. We'll just point our guns and fire at a solid, brown wall of shaggy critters. It'll be our last-ditch stand before we're overrun."

Quickly looking at his men, he asked, "Any questions?" Not waiting for replies, he growled, "Get your asses moving *pronto,* and make sure it's done in the time we have left!"

⬥

Hollering, waving hats, cracking whips, and using their horses, Jonah and Frank ran the remuda and livestock over the northern hills. They enlisted nine other riders to help them, as they rode down the line of wagons. Milk cows and oxen were the slowest, but before long, the entire remuda was beyond the crest of the first hill.

"Keep them headed north," Jonah commanded, as he saw Frank sharply swerve his horse to keep a straggler moving. "The wind is coming our way, so there'll be little chance of our animals catching the buffaloes' scent."

When they were sufficiently distant, Jonah signaled to the others to slow down. "We'll hold them here and keep them milling around in a circle. Let's get them really tired, so they won't think of rushing off. Frank, you and I'll ride back to the ridge, where we can see below. If the stampede changes direction and comes this way, we'll return. You fellows stay with the animals. And let me make one thing very clear, if any animal bolts—shoot it. Is that understood?"

The men, mostly farmers on their way to plow virgin lands out West, were shocked into silence, their faces blank, trying to understand a command that ran counter to the very grain of their being.

Seeing the dubious expressions, he quickly explained, "We have them out of the way up here above the valley. Yet, if they are rattled by the stampede, it's better to lose a few than the whole lot. Now, do you get my meaning?"

Finally seeing nods, young Frank said, "Let's ride, big brother."

As they reached the edge of the ridge, Jonah figured there was little chance that the buffalo would swerve and come up the steep hills. He had seen small numbers of buffalo often in Missouri, and the train had even stopped a week earlier to hunt on the edge of a large herd, adding fresh meat to their supplies. He and his brother had been part of the hunting party, as they were experienced hunters with rifles. But Frank possessed the keenest shooting eye.

Time dragged by slowly, as the young men looked westward, watching the approaching brown cloud of dust and hearing the deep, menacing rumble of thousands of hooves tearing up the ground.

Reaching for his pocket watch, Jonah commented dryly, "They're right on schedule, just as the captain predicted." Looking eastward, he saw the distant lines of wagons. Those forming the arrow-point were nearly in place, and men were already driving unhitched teams between the parallel lines of prairie schooners. "No question now, they're coming along our fork of this basin," he said, dismounting. Startled, he added, "Frank, quick, get off your horse. The ground is shaking under my boots."

"Well, I'll be," his brother said, as he stepped off his mount. "That's got to be one large herd coming this way."

A huge dust cloud, resembling a brown fog, filled the western sky. It rolled forward like tumbleweed before a brisk wind, yet it was contained by the hills bordering the sides of the valley.

Jonah detected the shaggy heads of the lead animals emerging at the front of the cloud, dark curly hair blending into the rising dust, broken only by the thin sheen of nearly foot-long horns. He knew that the largest of the monsters weighed up to a ton, with the big bulls standing over six feet high and measuring a dozen feet long. Looking toward the train again, he noted that everything was in place. *Even now,* he figured, *settlers are taking aim behind the lead wagons, guns pointed toward the advancing danger.*

Frank leaned toward his brother, shouting to be heard. "I feel helpless up here on the ridge. Surely, there's something more we can do? Without some way to turn the stampede, they're heading straight for the wagons, and I fear that our folks will be flattened by these four-legged critters."

Jonah studied the herd's progress, and the lay of the land below. Over countless decades, rain and snow runoff from the surrounding hills had formed gullies, scarring the basin floor, which ran toward the meandering river on the far side. The uneven terrain forced the main body of animals to slow, allowing the leaders to pull ahead by forty or fifty yards.

Frantic, Frank shouted to be heard, "Our train is going to be overrun, sure as night follows day."

Making a decision, Jonah loudly commanded, "Get on your horse, little brother, and follow me." Swinging up on the saddle quickly and spurring his animal hard, he plunged over the steep embankment. His mount literally slid down on its hindquarters, trying to maintain its balance, with Jonah doing the same, until both reached a wide ledge running below the crest. Reining in, he dismounted and turned to watch his brother descend the treacherous hill.

"Whew, that's some ride," Frank hooted, jumping off his horse. Watching the approaching stampede, he shouted, "Good God Almighty, nothing can stop them brutes."

Loudly, Jonah answered, "Soon, the leaders will be below and opposite where we're standing. What do you reckon the shooting range will be?"

Gauging it with an experienced eye, Frank replied, "About a hundred yards, give or take."

"That's about what I make it. You're the best shooter, with your Hawken .50-caliber rifle. When they come in range, you knock down as many of the leaders as you can. I'm hoping they'll pile up, creating a barrier to split the herd. You won't have much time, and you'll have to reload after each shot, so I'll also leave my rifle with you. That way, you may get off three, or perhaps, four shots before the leaders are out of range. Think you can hit them from this distance?"

"I'll surely try. What're you figuring to do?"

"I'm going to ride down to the bottom and, using my bullwhip, I'll try to turn them towards the river on the south side of the train. If that doesn't work, I'll use my six-shooter."

"Damnation, big brother, if your horse fails, that herd will flatten you like squashed gooseberry pudding. And to boot, you could be shot by our own folks, when you near the wagons. If that ain't bad enough, those shaggy beasts will gore you with their black horns, if they get a chance."

"I know all that, but it's the only thing that comes to mind." Jonah acknowledged, handing over his rifle.

As the streaming stampede advanced beneath the brown cloud, the thumping noise increased, becoming thunderous, with a heart-pounding intensity that over-whelmed and assaulted their ears, right down to the very core of their souls.

Rearing, their horses pulled hard on their reins, wide-eyed with fear.

Frank stared at his brother, then gave him an awkward bear hug. "God be with you," he hollered.

Jonah's hands trembled with adrenalin-stoked excite-ment, as he started to mount. At the same instant, his edgy horse began galloping before his foot found the stirrup. Grimly, he hung from the pommel, while trying to lope alongside, until he firmly planted his left foot on the ground and used the horse's momentum to swing himself up into the saddle. Reining his stallion about hard, he returned to his brother.

Exhilarated, he yelled, "If anything happens to me, tell Tennie Possard back at the train that my last words were for her." With that, he saluted smartly, reined sharply left down the hill, and whipped the flanks of his horse with his hat. "Good luck to us all," he shouted, followed by howling his Indian yell, "*Yeooowee!*"

He and his horse made it to the bottom, beneath the rolling cloud of dust. Looking to his right, the fast-moving herd appeared to be an unending mass, and an awesome display of unstoppable brute force, stretching far into the haze. For a moment, he had an overpowering urge to turn around and climb up the slope.

Instead, he whirled his horse toward the stampede. It balked until Jonah, reins held tightly and spurs raking the animal's ribs, angled it toward the terrifying horde.

The dark eyes of the leaders focused straight ahead, their heads slightly lowered, ears laid back, and running at a twenty-mile-an-hour tempo pace. If they noticed him, there was no sign.

Good God, these animals aren't going to change direction just because I'm cracking my whip, he suddenly realized. *I have to ride with them, or they'll run right over me.* The young man's hands were sweaty inside his leather gloves, as he swerved the horse and began moving with the streaming torrent of animals. *Can I outrun the leaders?* Worried, he urged his horse faster over the uneven ground.

Closing on the menacing bulls in the lead, the task he set for himself became increasingly daunting. The distinctive dark humps on their shoulders were clearly visible, while large clods of sod flew back, ripped from the earth by the buffalos' flying hooves. He lashed out with his bullwhip, and repeatedly bellowed his Indian yell, "*Yeooowee,*" yet, it was lost amid the din of pounding hooves.

Frantically looking up, he saw the line of wagons approaching rapidly. *How in blue blazes am I going to turn them?* His whip fairly danced in his right hand, snapping and biting at the air. Making a decision, he discarded the whip and swerved his horse again, riding directly at the leading bull, and at that instant, he saw the animal turn his head slightly toward him.

"*Yeooowee!*" he roared once more to the wind. "At least, he knows we're coming. Well, horse, I hope you're prepared to meet your Maker, because we're going to ram that monster," he shouted, galloping swiftly toward the big black hump, thumbing one shot after another from his small-caliber six-shooter into the mass of dirty brown hair.

Closing the distance swiftly, the young man gave a final tug on his sweat-stained hat and, at the last moment, tightly gripped the saddlebow's pommel with both gloved hands.

The next instant, the big bull flung its massive head toward them, burying a horn deeply in his horse's straining biceps. The vicious collision sent Jonah flying head-over-heels, until he landed and rolled on the ground. Both animals died instantly and toppled to the earth in a skidding heap of broken bodies.

Momentarily dazed, he looked up at the quickly approaching wall of black hooves. Instinctively, he dived behind the fallen animals for shelter, flattening himself, yet there was scant protection from the on-coming wave of death.

A split-second later, a buffalo hurdled over him, while others split to the sides. The thundering noise and dust overwhelmed him, as the ground shook violently. There was nothing else to do but wait for his inevitable fate.

Another animal leaped over the blockade, as did several others in quick succession. However, the rapid pace of events became a blur to him. The next one nearly cleared, but at the last moment, its forefoot caught on the hump of the downed buffalo. The big bull lost its balance and somersaulted to the ground just beyond terror-stricken Jonah.

At once, some of the tightly packed bison dodged while others, unable to swerve, plowed into the carcasses. An unstoppable reaction followed, with one-after-another colliding with the tangled mass, as the large wall of maimed and dying animals quickly grew higher and broader.

Stunned, he saw sweaty animals lying everywhere and felt the heavy impact of still more four-footed bodies slamming into the increasingly impenetrable barricade of death. In the distance, he heard the faint crack of gunfire, yet couldn't be sure, as the ground continued to vibrate beneath him, and his furry cave grew. The grunts and gasps of dying animals filled his ears, and the overpowering stench of sweat, dust, and pungent entrails—the smell of death—filled his senses. He lost conscious reality, accepting that his next breath would be his last. In the final fleeting moment of awareness, Tennie's face flashed before his eyes, calling and reaching out to him. Then, there was nothing.

Eva's Room
New Philadelphia

It was warm in the house, as Eva lay the letter aside and used the envelope to fan herself.

"Oh, the poor man," Viola cried. "What a terrible way to die, crushed beneath hairy critters like a bug under foot. Yet, how brave he was, and oh my word, so manly."

"Well, wipe away your tears and sobs, sister. He didn't die. This is what Frank says happened next," she said, returning to the letter.

"Unbelieving, I watched the growing wall of buffalo robes and was beside myself at the thought of losing my brother, as the wooly bodies engulfed him. Shooting a final round, I grabbed both rifles and mounted, sending my horse sliding down the hillside.

The mass of stampeding animals was veering off, far to the south side of the valley, and were already streaming wide of the arrowhead formation of wagons, but I stared in horror at the carnage looming before me ..."

Plains of Nebraska Territory

Frank was nearly overcome by guilt and the heavy weight of seeing his brother smothered by the buffalo carnage. *It's all my fault,* he chided himself, riding across the ground like the wind and losing his hat. *If I hadn't decided to run away from the farm, my brother wouldn't be lying beneath that pile of stinking buffalo. But good old Jonah, he wouldn't let me run off for Oregon Territory alone. He's always been there when I needed him.*

Near the tangled mountain of animals, Frank slid his horse to a halt and jumped off. "Jonah!" he shouted. "Big brother, can you hear me? Are you alive? Say something. Please, let me hear your voice." Without regard to the death throes of flailing legs, he climbed on top of the bodies.

He heard a roar and glanced at the wagon train, as the settlers—every man, woman, and child—abandoned their hiding places and ran toward the carcasses. They had just witnessed the most terrifying event of their lives, as they shouted thanks for having been spared. Captain Ernie led the crowd, riding low in the saddle and urging his horse faster.

"Jonah," Frank called, clambering over the dead bison and trying to avoid the involuntary kicks of unwinding muscles. "Jonah! Big brother, say something! I want to believe that you're alive. Please, let me hear you call out."

Faintly, seemingly from a great distance, he heard something. Excited, he shouted, "Against all odds, it has to be him." He stood on the mountain of animals, pale and shaken from the fast-paced events, yet he was now hopeful. As the train captain dismounted, he said, "I think I hear Jonah calling from over here somewhere."

As Shep rode up, the captain ordered, "Ride back to the train, quick-like. Bring half a dozen axes, two or three sets of block and tackle, and a couple of harnessed teams. And get some men to help you. Then, get back here fast, so we can unearth what's left of the brave lad from beneath this pile of hides."

At that moment, a large bull staggered to its feet, with sharp horns glistening, lowered his head and prepared to gore and trample the captain. Three gunshots from Shep and others ended the threat as the animal toppled heavily to its knees, gave a last snort, and rolled on its side. Soon, other guns were firing, as men stilled the twitching animals.

New Philadelphia

Eva rearranged her skirts, shuffled to the next page, and continued reading.

"Despite the havoc, Jonah was alive, the Lord be praised, yet unconscious. There were no broken bones and only a few scratches to show for his escapade. We took him to the nearest wagon, and as it happened, it belonged to Tennie Possard's family, the girl who was constantly on his mind.

We carefully laid him in the wagon, with Tennie cushioning his head on her lap. She called his name and wiped his dirt-streaked face with a damp cloth. Slowly, my brother stirred himself and, finally, with eyes half-opened, he asked what had happened to the train. We told him, and the girl, bending over him, began praising his brave deeds.

I saw a grin begin to form on Jonah's face, and I knew that he was fine. Then, the fool asked the darndest question. He wondered if it would be all right with everyone if he just laid there with his head on Tennie's lap, all the way to Oregon.

I would have punched him, except I was laughing too hard with relief."

Both Eva and Viola laughed, holding their sides, as tears rolled down their cheeks.

Eva finally asked, "Can you imagine Frank's happiness and the cheekiness of his brother, resting his head on that young woman?"

"I'd give anything to have one of those buffalo robes," Viola answered, smoothing her blue dress. "That's the most thrilling tale I've ever heard. It simply takes my breath away. What exciting times those boys had. Ev, you must read me another letter. They're too precious to miss."

"Well, there are more, but for now, I have to leave for work. I'll read another time when we're together. Viola, you have to promise me that all this stays between you and me. If Father ever got wind of this letter-writing thing, you know he'd blow up with anger and then harangue me."

"My dear, you're not only my kin, you're also my closest friend. You can talk to me about anything. I'm always here when you need me."

"Thank you, dear sister."

CHAPTER FOUR

New Philadelphia

Sitting in her room, Eva thought about the adventures that Frank and his brother had encountered. Picking up a pen, she began writing her response to her pen pal's last letter.

February 24, 1888

Dear Frank,

Your recent letter was so welcome. I look forward to each and then I can't rest until the answer is in the mail.

The weather here is still very cold, and the newspaper reports blizzards have hit many states. Current information is now passed along by telegraph wires. How did we learn about such events before? I guess, we just didn't know.

My work at the library keeps me busy indoors, and out of the miserable weather. I love thumbing through the books that we receive every month.

Your new cabin sounds like it will be sizeable. How many rooms will it have? Will there be a loft? Is it located deep in the woods or on a hill? By the way, what prompted you to build new quarters?

My eldest sister, Mary, is expecting her third baby this winter, and she and her husband are excited. My younger sisters scat about like bees after honey. Their energy seems inexhaustible. I also think about the sister and brother who were taken from us by the illness that hit our area a few years ago. It's so sad. They both had their whole lives before them. It reminds me that life is fragile, and everyone should make the most of theirs.

Viola, my next oldest sister, is my closest friend. I hope you don't mind, but once in a while, I read a portion of your letters to her. We just finished going through the one where you and Jonah confronted the stampeding herd of buffalo. As Viola said, you boys certainly had exciting adventures on your journey west. And what risks you took!

I so yearn to see more of the world. You must be so thankful that you took the opportunity to travel across our big country. How was it that you and your brother decided to run off from your father's farm in Missouri? Was it only the exciting thought of adventures?

Enclosed is a recent picture of me that a local man photographed. After all this time, I thought you might be curious about the lady who sends you letters. As you can see, I'm no raving beauty, yet I hope it doesn't frighten you and stop you from continuing to write. Is it possible for you to send me your picture? I would like that very much.

Affectionately yours,

Eva

Eva's correspondence with the "wild man," as her sister referred to Frank Sommer, began six months earlier. During a meeting of the ladies attending the *Friends of the Library Association*, Mrs. Shott read a clipping from the big newspaper to the north, *The Cleveland Plain Dealer*. It described the dire shortage of marriage-aged females in the remote northwest corner of the American frontier, and the many lonely men seeking wives.

The article went on to say how successful some had become as a result of their mining, forestry, and fishing efforts, and what wonderful providers they were for the more adventurous woman who was brave enough to make the trip.

Eva was captivated by the thought of traveling across thousands of miles to the western frontier. *I'm envious of folks whose lives are filled with adventure, while establishing new homesteads, far away from the unexciting routine here in New Philadelphia, Ohio.*

Halfway through, Mrs. Shott stopped reading for a moment, gauging the level of the group's interest, and hoping that she had not selected a boring topic. Nothing was further from the truth. Noticing this, the woman read the entire article, word-for-word. It ended with an address for *The Mercer Girls*, a foundation sponsored by Mr. Asa Shinn Mercer, the first president of the Territory University of Washington. His group placed advertisements in newspapers, seeking single Christian women who were willing to travel and work in the territory as teachers, clerks, and other respectable occupations.

The organization also fostered letter writing between women in eastern states and men located in the most remote parts of Washington Territory, in order "to quiet the hearts and souls of the brave and lonely men on the frontier." Finally, the foundation offered to forward any letters it received. Mrs. Shott ended her talk by proposing that the library association adopt such a correspondence project as a community-spirited endeavor.

Well, Eva recalled, *you would have thought that the world had stood on its head at the stirrings this suggestion caused, what with all the busy-bee discussions going on and the level of tittering from more than one attendee. There seemed to be a curious energy in the room, amid sly smiles, a few smirks, and protests.*

Several ladies rose to a point of order, offering various views. One expressed outrage, saying, "Writing letters to cheer up shaggy-headed and wildly raucous men is offensive to a lady's sensibilities in this day and age."

Another voiced the opinion that the program sounded like a lark, and it certainly would be a more enjoyable way to pass the time, rather than playing silly parlor games, like charades.

A gray-haired woman slowly stood, with the help of her cane. She was clearly upset. "You ladies beware," she warned. "Temptation for civilized women comes in many forms. Writing letters to strange men sounds just like the kind of trap the devil sets to draw some of you into licentious goings-on."

There were audible gasps from more than one lady, and a few snickered.

Eva was far from amused. *Good heavens, the balderdash from some of these "civilized ladies" is really very thick and heavy today,* she thought, cynically surveying the group.

However, most of the attendees that day agreed that the lonely, brave men would lead happier lives, if only their group took pity and shared a kind and sympathetic word. Indeed, a lively cord was struck by Mrs. Shott's reading.

Finally, Mrs. Hagadorn, the chairwoman, summed up the sentiments by saying she favored the idea, as it provided an enlightened and compassionate undertaking for the association.

Many remained silent, and Eva noticed that some wore a wily smile, perhaps masking the fanciful titillation of communicating with a strange man on the edge of civilization, while keeping it secret from their world in New Philadelphia. *That would be a great plot for a Mary Elizabeth Braddon novel,* she thought, and she smiled at the notion.

Eva was keen about the idea, and she signed up, using the library's address to avoid the eyes of busybodies at home. Ten weeks later, the first letter from Frank Sommer arrived.

She never learned how her letter was directed to him. Yet, she awaited a reply with an eagerness that was unsettling. Unable to keep her pen pal to herself, she confided in Viola shortly after receiving the second letter.

Her sister's interest grew, and she became almost as engaged in the exchanges as Eva, often imploring her to retell Frank's stories and adventures.

CHAPTER FIVE

Days became weeks, as Eva continued working and exchanging letters with Frank. Each time a letter arrived, she marveled at the speed of the mail service. The transcontinental rail line had been completed some twenty years earlier, and freight, people, and mail moved at a pace that was unimaginable before the Civil War. An overland trip from Chicago to San Francisco took only ten days, compared with six months for early pioneers traveling by wagon over the trails to California.

On a springtime Sunday in May, Eva and Viola packed a picnic lunch and found a grassy knoll overlooking the Tuscarawas River. It was rare for them to have an afternoon to themselves, and the occasion was a treat.

"It seems strange to be sitting out here without your family along," Eva commented. She spread a quilt on the grass and, fluffing her daisy-colored skirts, seated herself with a modicum of grace. Looking around, she loosened the tie string on the yellow ruffles holding the neck of her dress, as the day was warm, even in the shade.

Viola sat opposite and opened the basket. She offered a fried chicken leg to her sister and eagerly asked, "C'mon, Ev, don't keep me in suspense. What's the news from that wild man?" The hues of her dress matched her eyes, as she arranged her skirt. Taking off her white bonnet, she reached for a carrot and began nibbling. Turning again to her sister, she was suddenly concerned. "Ev, why do you look so sad? Oh, something terrible has happened, hasn't it? I can read it on your face. Talk to me! "

"Well, it's sad. In my last letter, I asked him if there was any other reason for him and his brother to leave Missouri. He admits that part of it was the sheer adventure of seeing different lands. I guess he and I have similar feelings about exploring."

"You always were the one to try new things, Ev. I envy your high-spirited, inquisitive nature."

"What are you implying, sister? Are you saying that I'm a nosey woman?"

Impatiently, her sister asked, "Did your Mr. Frank and his brother have any other pressing reason for hightailing it out West?"

Becoming serious, Eva said, "There was another, at least for Frank. He had fallen in love."

"He's married? Oh, good God Almighty, I feared something like this would turn up."

"No, silly, he was sweet on a girl who lived on a neighboring farm in Missouri, only to have his heart broken."

"I knew there had to be something else."

"It seems that he and the girl were together as much as possible, yet they were both young and hadn't given much thought to the future. Then, one day she disappeared. He was beside himself with worry, and no one would tell him where she had gone."

"Ev, I don't think I like where this is going."

"Weeks later, the girl returned and, surprisingly, he heard that she and her family were coming for a meal after Sunday church services. As you can imagine, he was beside himself with happiness. He said in his letter that he felt something was amiss when she arrived. The families sat down and, after prayers, an announcement was made that the girl was going to be married."

"My, that must have shocked him. So, who was she going to marry?"

"Frank's father."

"Good Lord in heaven above! Wait, didn't you say she was young?"

"Yes, she was fifteen at the time, and his papa was fifty years old. Can you imagine?"

"Are you joshing me?" Viola responded in amazement. "His father married his sweetheart?"

"Yep."

"How in the world does a man his age court a girl who is that young? And wasn't he already married? I still don't understand."

"His first wife had died the prior year from the ague that swept through their valley. At the time, the family had ten children, and nine were living at home."

"My, his father was prolific and obviously liked snuggling at night. Still, I'll ask again, how does a fifty-year-old man court a young girl?"

"Hold onto your corset, because there are more twists to this tale. You're right, Frank was stunned at the news. Later, he confronted the girl alone. Only then did he learn that she had gone to her granny's farm to recuperate, after being beaten and raped by a farmhand."

"How horrible for her."

"And while she was away, she learned that she was with child."

"Oh, the poor girl."

"Unbelievably, Frank says her folks shunned her, fearing that their small farming community would accuse them of following ungodly ways."

"I can't believe what you're telling me. How she must have suffered."

"Further, her parents strongly pushed her into the marriage with Frank's father."

"Life sure has unexpected moments, doesn't it?"

"You haven't heard the last of it, sister dear. The marriage arrangement was made by the girl's pa. And that resulted in the man's mortgage being canceled."

"Oh, c'mon, Ev, are you telling me that there was also a bank involved in this tangled muddle?"

"Nope. Years earlier, the land was sold to the girl's family by Frank's father, and he held the mortgage."

"Wait, let me get this straight" Viola said, looking confused. "You're saying that Frank's papa . . ." Biting her lip and hesitating for a moment, she continued, "His father made the arrangement with the girl's parents by canceling their mortgage. Isn't that like buying . . .?"

Nodding, Eva interrupted, "There probably were other reasons involved, like the girl knowing that she and the baby had a home. And, in truth, his father may not have known anything about the attraction between the two young people. Yet, Frank's view is much like the one that you're thinking."

"Lordy, that's a bizarre yarn. Lend me your handkerchief, Eva. I'm tearing up again. Well, at least there was someone to care after them."

"Frank writes that he'll never forgive his pa for ruining his life. Anyway, he couldn't stand living in the small Missouri community any longer and decided to run away. His brother joined him for the adventure, and as a way to look out for him."

Viola simply stared at her sister, as she wiped her cheeks and blew her nose.

"When I read his letter," Eva said, "I cried, too, for all the hurt and agony it must have caused them. Lastly, he says that there has been no other woman in his life."

Brightening and with an impish smile on her face, Viola responded, "I've said it before, and I'll say it again, this fellow has been lonely for too long."

Eva stared pensively at the horizon. Finally, she asked, "Would you like to hear more about their adventures traveling along the Oregon Trail?"

"Indeed, I'd love it. His letters are so thrilling. It's almost as though I'm sharing the experience with them. And for that, you can have another piece of chicken."

"Thank you very much. I'm really hungry today." Wiping her hands on a napkin, she continued. "This adventure occurred after the buffalo stampede, as the wagon train neared Fort Laramie, in Wyoming Territory. Let me read his words."

"March 22, 1888

Dearest Eva Mae,"

With a sly grin, her sister butted in, "Oh my, now it's 'dearest,' is it?" Well, that's new. What comes next? Maybe it'll be darling or perhaps even sweetheart or love of my life or . . ."

"Oh, hush," Eva responded, chuckling. "Now, listen and don't be such a smart-mouth."

"Your image arrived today along with a clip of your hair, and I cannot tell you how thrilled I am."

"You sent him a picture of yourself? And a lock of hair? This writing is becoming a serious undertaking for you, isn't it?"

"Will you please be still, so I can read?" Waiting a moment, she continued.

"You are even prettier than I imagined, with your reddish-brown hair and beautiful eyes. I'm much obliged to you. I'll treasure and keep both with me always."

"H'mm."
"Shhh!"

"It's not easy for me to have a daguerreotype taken out here at the edge of the wilderness, however, I'll look for someone who has the equipment, perhaps at the university in Seattle. I need to travel there anyway to file my claim for the land where I am building. I'm neither dashing nor handsome, and I hope you won't be too disappointed.

I long for the day that we finally meet. Do you think it will ever happen? I often wonder. Have you given any thought about traveling and seeing new places, like the beautiful land here in Washington? I would love to show you the area and the rivers I fish, as well as the 'Colt 45' gold mine where I have a stake. Perhaps you can let me have your thoughts in your next letter. I find myself thinking about you all the time and especially in the still of the night. I'm a private man, but everyone needs someone. Don't you agree?"

Once more, Viola interrupted, "Ev, this man is in love with you."

Astonished, she asked, "How could he be? We've never met, and he's only just seen my picture for the first time."

"My dear, all you have to do is *really* read the words in his letter. It sure sounds to me like he's expressing some very deep affection for you. And if it isn't love now, it soon will be."

"Dear sister, you're very intuitive, yet you're also such a tease. Maybe I should teach you a lesson about interrupting people by stopping and putting this letter away for today."

"Don't you dare!"

"My dear, no more interruptions, or else!"

"The walls of the new cabin are up. A group of my friends helped me raise the sides over a ten-day period. I had already cut the logs to length and notched the ends. We rigged two hoists, using nearby trees to mount block and tackle. For the tallest sections of the walls, we created a ramp and, with hemp ropes wound around a log, we heaved and lifted each into place.

With the favorable weather holding, we also laid down smaller limbs for the roof. I am pleased that I've been able to accomplish much so early in the year. And, to answer your questions, there will be three rooms—a large great room plus two others. Yes, there will be a loft just like the one me and my brothers and sisters slept in, when we were young. I look forward to a time when it serves the same purpose for my children."

Viola threw up her hands in mock horror. "Land sakes alive, now youngsters are on his mind. What do you suppose he's really thinking when he writes to you about his future children?"

"The man is simply pouring out his dreams. Why can't you just accept that? And, in building a new home, he's properly thinking ahead. I'd say that's a fine quality."

"Uh-huh. And when did he take it into his head to build this new dwelling? I wonder if it was about the same time that you began writing to him?"

"Oh, Viola, you're just a rabble-rouser."

"Read on, dear sister, read on."

"All right, but once again, I remind you that you have to be still in order to be a good listener. In fact, if you had just shown a tiny bit of patience, Frank goes on to answer your question. Here's what he says.

"By the way, I began building it because my existing dugout dwelling keeps flooding inside, whenever it rains hard. The floor is about three feet below ground level, with a structure and roof above. I trenched around the outside to handle the runoff water, but this proved inadequate. So, I started planning for the new log cabin, and this time, there is no sunken floor.

You asked about my family's roots and the adventure we had on our journey west. I gather your sister is also showing an interest in my tales. So, I'll happily oblige.

My folks are from Holmes County, Ohio, the next county west of yours. At some point, our ancestors came from overseas, most likely from the Lower Palatinate area of Europe, somewhere along the Rhine River. I was born in Seneca, Missouri in the year of our Lord, 1839. This part of Missouri is called the land of the Six Bulls, named by one of the original pioneers. It is a small community with farms dotting the area.

About our adventures, we had a parcel. We actually left the wagon train when it was about a third of the way along the Oregon Trail. What happened next changed the rest of our lives, but I am getting ahead of myself. I'll pick up from the last letter, as we neared Fort Laramie.

Captain Ernie called a meeting of all the folks in the train. Neither Jonah nor I had any idea what was coming . . ."

CHAPTER SIX

Oregon Trail
Wyoming Territory

Frank shifted from foot to foot. He was not sure why everyone was called to the late afternoon meeting. Some folks appeared uneasy, as though they expected a warning of some danger ahead. *Perhaps, a storm is coming*, he reasoned, *although the skies seem clear.*

"Settle down," Captain Fudge commanded, raising his voice to be heard by the nearly five hundred people in the train. To be seen by everyone, he stood on a box, as most folks formed a circle, sitting on the ground or standing, while others minded unruly youngsters.

Frank found a place at the back with his brother.

"This meeting won't take long, and then we can get on with our evening supper," the captain said. "Since leaving Fort Kearney, we've continued following the Platt River and passed Courthouse Rock, Chimney Rock, and Scotts Bluff. I saw many of you carving your names on the side of the bluff. And, who knows, maybe someday your kin and friends will see the scratching and know that you journeyed this way.

"We've already faced difficulties that have tested our will and faith. Now, we have a different kind of struggle ahead of us. Our travels, so far, have been over mostly level prairie, and that's nearly at an end. You all know that, ahead of us, there'll be tall mountains to cross. And I assure you, they'll be the biggest and highest ones that you've ever seen, with steep grades going up and treacherous descents to greet us on the downside.

"In a few days, we'll reach Fort Laramie in Wyoming Territory, and it'll mark the completion of one-third of our journey to Oregon. We'll lay over at the fort for three or four days, making repairs, resting, and restocking supplies.

"As more settlers travel across this great country of ours, this garrison is the most important army post west of the Mississippi River. It began as a fur-trading outpost, and it's been a part of the army's western string of forts for many years. You can do some restocking at the store, but be forewarned, prices will be sky-high. It takes a heap of effort to bring supplies this far west, and you'll find that folks at the fort are right good at charging for it.

"When we leave Fort Laramie, it'll mark the beginning of our passage through some of the most rugged mountains that I expect you've ever seen. They're also some of the finest looking, rising up sky-high, and some have snow atop the year around. We'll follow the Sweetwater River for a fair distance. As it curls about, we'll have to ford it several times. If rainstorms are about, we'll float the wagons across, using good-sized logs lashed to the sides of the wagons. The Sweetwater will take us through a cleft in the mountains called Devils Gate, which points us exactly toward South Pass. It's the only route through the big mountains where wagons can cross.

"Once in the pass, we'll travel along a broad valley between the peaks. The pass is deceiving, as the upslope is somewhat gentle, for the most part. Many of you will only know we're climbing because you'll be easily winded."

One settler shouted, "Captain Fudge, are you telling us that it's going to be an easy passage?"

The wagon train leader looked at the man for a moment before speaking, his expression serious. "Just the opposite, and that's the rub. While the climb will seem reasonable to you, your teams will be wearing out before your eyes, pulling your heavy loads."

Another man asked, "So, what are you suggesting?"

"It's very simple. Many of your wagons in this train continue to be overloaded. Shep and I cautioned you back in Independence, and I'm telling you like it is, as we're nearing the climbing part of our journey. You need to lighten your loads. And while South Pass is a reasonable climb, other soaring mountain passes with much steeper grades are three hundred miles farther west. You have to wonder if your draft animals can survive. And if they fail, you and your family may be hard-pressed to stay alive."

Frank was not expecting such a somber warning, and it seemed to stun the group. Many had started the long journey east of the Mississippi River, having come from every state and territory in the nation. Others crossed the seas before beginning the trip. All were drawn by the irresistible call of available land, adventure, riches, and a chance to build new lives on the American frontier. He sensed a feeling of anxiety in the crowd.

The silent hush was jolted by the captain's next order. "Now hear me good, because I'm only going to say this one more time. When we reach the fort, I expect all of you to have in mind those things that really aren't necessities for your survival during the remainder of our journey. The rest has to be abandoned. Outside the fort, you'll soon see a pile of discards from other trains that have come before us. Those earlier folks were faced with the same choices that you'll be making."

Neither Frank nor his brother was affected by the order, yet Frank felt sorry for folks in the train who would have to part with cherished belongings.

"I'm not discarding my grandma's pedal-pump organ," one woman wailed."

The captain simply shrugged. "If it's not important to the survival of you and your stock, leave it."

"My animals are doing well," a balding man stated. "We've had good grass for grazing up to this point, and they show it."

"Maybe you're hearing me, Mr. Tish, but you're not grasping the seriousness of my meaning. I've been over this trail many times, and I'm telling you what's going to happen. Heavy, overloaded wagons will kill your teams, just as sure as putting a gun to their heads. We'll be climbing over the very backbone of this whole, dadgum nation. Make your choice! Keep your heavy, sentimental crap and kill your animals, or hang onto only what you need and give yourself a better chance to stay alive."

"We have spare draft animals in the remuda," a man named Story persisted. He stood in front of the captain as he angrily spoke. "Why can't we just relieve our teams by rotating them more often?"

Frank saw the color rise in the captain's face. *I think he's about to get downright angry. Folks know what he's saying is true, but they're having difficulty accepting it.*

Ernie Fudge took off his hat, beating it against his leg for a moment to remove trail dust. His reddish-colored hair glistened in the late-afternoon sun as he slowly did a full turn, looking over the crowd. His face was somber and his eyes narrowed. Finally, he seemed to heave a sigh. "Excuse my language, ladies," he roared, "but damnation and fiery brimstone from hell, some of you folks still aren't paying attention to my meaning. Spare animals are just that, extras when a mule or ox fails. We'll still have some that'll break a leg, get snake-bit, or go lame with split hooves."

"But some of the things have been in our family for generations," a woman at the rear of the crowd cried out. "We know that they can't be replaced in the new land."

"I'm sorry, ma'am, and what you say is true enough," Captain Fudge answered.

Frank saw the train leader pause and look at the many that were in his care on this long and dangerous journey. His face was tinged with redness, and Frank knew he was frustrated.

Raising his voice, Captain Fudge spoke angrily, "My duty is to get everyone of you to Oregon City, and that means getting you there alive. That takes fit animals, and by thunder, that's what we're going to do!" Delivering his last words with force and strength, he pounded a fist into the palm of his other hand with brisk finality, to signal the end of further discussion. "And by damn, that's an order. Do it!"

Frank looked at his brother, who shrugged.

———◆———◆———

Eva paused with her letter reading and gazed across the broad expanse of water. "It's a lovely day, lounging here, isn't it? I love this time of year and seeing all the blooms."

"Yes, it's my favorite time, too," Viola replied. "Everything feels fresh, and the blossoming trees are a grand picture of beauty, particularly the dogwood. Everything is budding, yet the weather hasn't turned sultry." Pausing, she looked quickly at her sister. Wagging her finger, she added, "Now don't be changing the subject to blossoms and the weather. Tell me what happens next."

"All right, but first I'm going to have another piece of chicken."

"Eat fast."

"You do have to stop interrupting me," Eva chided.

"*Well*, I beg your pardon," Viola commented in mock anger. "You're the one that's eating. I, on the other hand, will try to maintain my dignity, while retaining full control of my wild and uninhibited self during this glorious day." She giggled at her exaggerated elocution. "Want some salt? Now, will you please just get on with it?"

Gulping down her food and with a quick laugh, Eva replied, "Fine, let's have no more comments. Frank writes:"

"*The captain asked Jonah and me to ride ahead to Fort Laramie and select a campsite for the train.*"

It was Sunday and a day for rest, as we followed the wagon train's routine of making at least one-hundred miles each week, paced by the slow-moving oxen. Many folks used the day to repair wagons, hunt for game, and to catch up on chores, like washing clothes.

Jonah went to say good-bye to Miss Tennie Possard, the apple of his eye, while I went hunting with men from the train. Golly, my brother was sure smitten with that green-eyed gal. This is what I learned the next day, as we were on the trail to Fort Laramie, and talking about . . ."

CHAPTER SEVEN

Wyoming Territory

Before setting off for the fort the following day, Jonah walked down the long line of wagons, trying to retain his composure before finding the Possard wagon.

Pa always said that it was best to let your thoughts breathe a little, instead of remaining buried in you. I'll know shortly if his advice works with Tennie.

The young woman was standing over a kettle of boiling water, stirring the contents with a thick wooden stick. She wore an apron over her gingham dress and few, if any, petticoats, considering the warm weather. Dusty, brown boots peaked from beneath the hem of her skirt.

"What're you fixing?" Jonah asked, awed to be in the presence of the pretty girl from Tennessee.

"Nothing you'd want," she replied. "I'm just boiling clothes, trying to get some of the dirt loose. They'll never be very colorful again. Everything is getting to look like plain old, trail-dust drab."

Unsure, Jonah nodded. "The captain asked me and Frank to ride ahead to select a campsite for the layover at Fort Laramie."

"Well, have a safe trip."

Hesitating until words came to him, he continued, "After we leave the fort, the next army post will be Fort Hall, where the California Trail splits off. Some folks are talking about leaving the train there and heading south to the California gold country."

"Oh?"

"Of course, we still have five or six weeks before reaching the turnoff."

"Is that so?"

"Frank and I've been thinking that we might go south and seek our fortune there."

The blonde-haired girl stopped stirring the boiling mess and stared at him for an instant. "And do what?"

"Well, we can find work in the gold mines or strike out on our own, looking for nuggets and glitter."

"Hogwash!"

Jonah was surprised at her quick and strong reaction.

Hot from standing over the boiling kettle, she continued, stirring the pot faster. "You'll end up like all of them other fools I've heard about, who mindlessly tramp over deserts, while going up and down mountains and living like aimless, wandering souls. They're ne'er-do-wells, that's what they are, every last one of them. And for what? Maybe you'd find a few grains of gold. And then, what becomes of the rest of your life? Don't you men have anything more on your minds, like ambitions to build things, raise families, or maybe cut out farmland from virgin territory? And, don't you want to make a mark with your life, rather than aimlessly trekking over hill and dale like meandering, itinerant fools."

Taken aback by the vigorous lecture, he said, "C'mon, Tennie, I know you and your family are bent on getting to Grants Pass in Oregon. Your pa has told me often that he's going into the lumber business. He has visions of building a new sawmill on the banks of the Rogue River, and if he's right, he'll get rich some day from the huge trees that grow like weeds in that country. That's his dream. Why can't I have one, too?"

"The thought of striking it rich is an appealing notion, except it's mired in claptrap. Going somewhere carpeted with forests sounds like a lot smarter idea to me than trying to stay clear of rattlesnakes while looking under rocks and waterfalls for a few specks of gold. Wouldn't you agree?"

He didn't know what the proper answer was, so he spoke from his heart. "Tennie, you know that I like you—a whole lot. You tended to me after my run-in with the buffalo, and I'm much obliged. If you'd just take some notice of me, I'd never leave you or the train."

"Look, Jonah, I've been plain and straight with you from the very first. You know my heart belongs to another back home in Tennessee. Before we left, he promised that he'd follow, when his affairs are settled. Nothing has changed my feelings for him."

"I see," Jonah mumbled. Downcast, he stared at the ground.

Hesitantly, Tennie continued. "Look, I admire you and your deeds. Your bravery during the stampede is something I'll always remember. As for tending to you afterwards, I was duty bound, as a lady brought up in a Christian tradition, to provide help and comfort."

I was a chore for her, and she was just doing her duty by looking after me, he thought, shouldering the crushing weight of her words. *And now, I'm making a fool of myself, lingering here like a suckling, moonstruck calf.* He looked at her with a steady gaze. "I can't change the deep feelings I have for you with some sleight of hand. I'd love to build a life with you in Oregon or California, or wherever the love in our hearts might have taken us, but I can see that it's not going to happen, and knowing it hits my soul with a couple of hard licks. I'll not carry on any more, and I apologize for any uneasiness or embarrassment that I have caused you. I can only assure you that you'll always remain in my memories."

Tennie blushed, as a loose strand of blonde hair fell down her cheek. Brushing it aside, she looked at him. Her wide-set, green eyes seemed to glow in a face gone pale. "I'm sorry," she said in a quiet voice. "Those are terribly sweet sentiments, but I'm telling you what's in my heart."

"I wish you all the best, and I hope that your life and love will be fulfilled someday." Turning, he walked away, holding his head high. But, his heart was broken and his stomach hurt with the gut-punched pain of rejected love.

New Philadelphia

Sitting on the banks of the Tuscarawas River, Eva's face had a far-away expression. She was swept up in the emotional hurt for Jonah, even though the event had occurred decades earlier.

Viola asked, "How in creation can she turn away such heartfelt love? I couldn't. His pleading would have simply melted my soul." With a dreamy expression, she whispered, "Please tell me what happened next."

Rousing herself, Eva continued.

"We had no trouble following the trail to the fort, as countless previous trains had deeply etched wagon

ruts in the hardpan dirt. Heavens, it was so obvious that a blind man would have had no difficulty following it.

The land had few lakes and rivers, and Jonah and I figured it wasn't suitable for farming, yet, surprisingly, the prairie grass was hip-high but nearly treeless. With so little wood, folks relied on dried buffalo chips for their fires. Most evenings, women and youngsters from the train collected the droppings, with one meal requiring as much as three full bushels.

We set out the next morning at first light, but my brother was moody and grumpy. I tried talking with him, but . . ."

CHAPTER EIGHT

Trail to Fort Laramie
Wyoming Territory

Jonah rode in silence, staring straight ahead, and lost in his thoughts. His hat was pulled low over his brow, as his horse plodded along.

"What ails you this morning?" Frank asked, as they followed the wagon ruts. "Here we are, free men on a beautiful morning, traveling across the high plains. And look at you, sitting your horse with a sour look on your face. Are you going to be a grouch-hog during this entire ride to the fort?"

Hearing no response, he continued, "I'll wager that you're thinking about that gal back at the train, aren't you? Surely, you remember Miss Tennessee Possard, the one with the prettiest green eyes this side of the Missouri River, don't you?" he teased.

Jonah showed no interest in his brother, and certainly not in the direction of his questions.

"C'mon," Frank urged. "What's it going to take to put a smile on your glum face, to replace that hang-dog look?"

"I'm not sure," Jonah replied.

"Well, big brother, we've both had poor starts with our womenfolk, haven't we? I guess us Sommer boys were born to be unlucky in love, as we have a hard time trying to establish harmonious relations with our women. Don't you agree?"

Finally smiling and then chuckling, Jonah replied, "We'll both have to be patient and wait for other times and more opportunities."

"I reckon."

"You do know that fair maidens aren't going to be plentiful where we're headed, don't you?"

"There ain't nothing I can do about that. Someday, I figure that will change and there'll be others."

Jonah was now laughing. "Some folks say that you can't get rid of a problem until you shuck it."

"That right? I don't think I've ever heard that rule."

"So, brother, let's start shucking."

"Amen, big brother, amen." Frank laughed as he said, "C'mon Jonah, let's make tracks for the outpost and see if you can leave your grumpiness in the dust behind us."

Three days later, they paused on a bluff, looking down at Fort Laramie, which was bustling with activity. It was the first sign of civilization they had seen since leaving Fort Kearney six weeks earlier.

Jonah pointed to the line of six, double-storied structures outlining the dusty parade grounds. "I reckon those buildings house the enlisted troopers. They likely sleep upstairs and have their gear and saddles below."

"Uh-huh. And those smaller ones near the center of the parade area must be for the officers," Frank added.

"By golly," Jonah said, standing in his stirrups, "would you look at the size of that horse barn over yonder."

"You're right. That's the biggest, longest barn I've ever seen."

Looking around the broad layout from their hillside advantage, Jonah observed, "I'm really surprised that this fort has no defensive walls around the perimeter, other than that small area, which might be the stockade."

As they rode down the hill, they rounded a stand of trees along the river and stopped, dumbfounded at the sight. Before them were huge areas littered with all manner of things, from household belongings to furniture and equipment of every sort. Some items appeared to be in reasonable shape, while others were weathered, warped, or in various stages of rust and deterioration.

"This must be the abandoned possessions that Captain Ernie described," Frank observed. "The number of items is really hard to believe. Heavens, the area must cover more than an acre."

"Everyone has dreams, and these things were once a part of the lives of folks who came this way."

"With all the money tied up in these discards, you'd think that someone would cart some of it away," Frank observed.

"Yep, you'd think that, except there are few people around for the next one thousand miles, north, south, east, or west, who need china washbasins, heavy wooden bedsteads, and the like." He knew that many settlers in the wagon train hoped that they could sell their overload items at the fort's trading post. Prices might be low, but at least it would be something.

Continuing toward the trading post, a sign outside the log building bluntly stated its rule.

WE SELL WHAT YOU NEED

WE DON'T BUY DISCARDS

NO EXCEPTIONS MADE

"Guess the fort trading post doesn't like competition," Frank commented.

"Well, if that don't beat all," Jonah replied. "You know, with the right outfit, we could make good money, hauling these discards west."

"Yep, except we don't have any wagons or draft animals or drivers," Frank pointed out. "And, least of all, we have no money."

The boys continued toward the river and located an area for the train's encampment. As they unsaddled the horses and laid out their bedrolls, it was obvious that the area had been used many times before.

Two days later, the train arrived at the fort, and Jonah saw the Possard wagon, with Tennie seated next to her mother.

As it passed him, the green-eyed woman turned away, avoiding his look by searching for something in the bed of the wagon behind her.

Once more, Jonah felt the crushing weight of rejection. *Now she's so annoyed with me that she pretends I don't exist. I reckon that really hurts the most.*

Brooding, he made his way toward the tree-lined river, resigned that nothing would ever come of his love for Tennie.

Loud yelling attracted his attention upriver, as two scruffy-looking men dragged an older fellow toward the water. The gray-haired man with the long beard resisted, loudly protesting. He had obviously consumed large quantities of whiskey and was fully in his cups.

"Now hear me good, you dirty, thieving scoundrels," the man yelled, slurring his words badly. "You'll not get any gold dust from me, or my name ain't Lem Spurgeon. Are you hearing me?"

"Shut your mouth, you old coot," one thief said, as they dumped the old man at the edge of the river. "We know you've prospected for gold in California and have a deep pouch hidden somewhere around here. We aim to have it. We also know you like to drink, so how about trying some water for a change? Let's see what happens when I hold your head under the river for a spell, Mr. Lem, you damn, cantankerous old cuss."

The two thieves rolled the protesting prospector deeper into the water, then ducked and held his head beneath for a considerable length of time, before letting him up for air.

Sputtering, Spurgeon took a deep, gasping breath. "You damn rascals, I won't give you . . ."

Again, his head went under.

Taken aback, it took Jonah a moment to gather his wits. Stooping, he picked up a large limb at the edge of the river and began running toward the three men. "You there," he shouted. "What're you doing to that man?" Sprinting at full speed, he saw that his words startled the two thieves.

One continued to keep the old man's face beneath the water, while the other turned toward Jonah, pulling a long knife from his waist. "Butt out! You're sticking your nose in private business, where it ain't fitting."

Quickly covering the distance, Jonah swung the tree limb mightily, catching the thief on the upper arm, staggering him. Yet, the man swiftly recovered.

Holding the blade low, the thief crouched and slashed upward.

The metal sliced through Jonah's shirtsleeve, just missing his arm. Once more, the young man brought the limb around, this time cracking it against the man's head and knocking him to the ground. Jonah turned toward the second thief, who released the prospector and drew his knife.

Rushing out of the river, the man feinted right and then came in under the swinging club, quickly thrusting the blade upward.

The knife sliced into Jonah's side. Grunting in pain, he once more raised the limb and brought it down with all his might across the thief's neck, splintering the wood.

By this time, the prospector was standing and swaying in the water, too tipsy to join the fight.

Both bandits had enough and scurried away.

Jonah dropped to his knees while holding his side, blood oozing between his fingers.

Prospector Lem Spurgeon knelt and laid him down, pressing a bandana against Jonah's side. "Young fellow," he mumbled, "you saved my life and my gold. I'm much obliged. I'm going to the fort for help. I'll be back pronto-quick."

Jonah closed his eyes, wondering how long it would take the old drunkard to stumble to the fort and return. Behind his closed eyes, the blonde-haired image of Tennie floated before his eyes.

At the fort infirmary, Jonah lay on a cot. A military doctor had tended him and closed the wound, saying the knife missed vital organs and that his recovery would take several weeks.

A sergeant had recorded his account of the attack, and fort soldiers were alerted. At the post, punishment for robbery was sixty days in a hot, sweltering hold. For attempted murder, convicted men were hanged.

On the third day, Captain Fudge stopped to see Jonah, removing his hat.

"How're you doing, son?"

"Better, thank you, sir."

"The doc says you'll be fine soon enough."

Jonah remained silent. Both he and Frank knew what was coming, having discussed the train's departure the prior evening.

"We'll be moving out, come morning," the captain continued. "You best get your rest and heal thyself. You can likely catch up with us before we get to Fort Hall."

"That's our thought, too, sir. We'll try."

"You and your brother have been a great help to me on this journey, and I want to thank you all for your hard work and your bravery. I know that you'll try to finish out the trip with us, but strange things can happen on the frontier. I've done the sums that you two have earned, and you deserve a little something extra," he said, fishing out two twenty-dollar gold pieces from his pocket.

"That's generous of you, sir," Jonah replied. "I'm sorry that we can't continue tomorrow. Frank and I hope to catch up and travel the trail with you folks again, at least to Fort Hall."

"You do that, son. We'll watch for you. Take care of yourselves, and Godspeed," Captain Fudge said, standing and putting his hat on. With a farewell salute, he departed.

Later in the day, Jonah dozed on the cot and gradually became aware that someone was standing near him. Opening his eyes, he was surprised to see Tennie.

"I hope I didn't wake you, but I didn't want to leave without saying good-bye," she said, in her soft tone of voice.

"The whole train has heard about what you did at the river. You just can't seem to stop doing courageous deeds, can you? Are you on the road to mending?"

"I have some pain in my side," he replied, struggling to sit up. But, I'm much better now that you're here."

"Oh, the way you talk," she answered with a blush. Her green eyes appeared almost luminous in the late-afternoon sun, as she stood looking down at him.

"I understand the train leaves in the morning."

"Yes. Pa wanted me to tell you that he hopes you recover soon and says he'll always remember what you and your brother did for everyone on the train."

"Please thank him and wish him well for me."

Timidly, she continued, as tears welled up in her eyes, "Jonah, I'm sorry I've been so hard on you. It's just that the fellow back home is never far from my thoughts."

Jonah remained silent.

Impulsively, Tennie sat on the edge of the cot and reached for his hand. "I wish things might have been different."

"Me, too, Tennie."

A tear slid slowly down her cheek, as she gripped his hand tightly. "You get yourself well, Jonah Sommer. I hope you boys can catch up with the train. As you know, my pa plans to settle us in Grants Pass, and if you're ever in the area, I hope you stop and see us."

"By golly, that sounds like an invitation."

"Well, of course it is," she said, smiling.

Glory be, he thought, more than a bit confused. *Is this beautiful gal saying she wants me to call on her in Oregon?*

"After all you've done for us and the other folks, you'll always be welcomed in our home."

"Oh."

"I mean," the girl quickly continued, "we'd be pleased to see you and your brother anytime you're out our way."

Looking at her for a moment, he said, "Well, thank you kindly for that gracious invitation. I'll keep it in mind."

He saw the hurt on her face from his curt remark. *Maybe our parting will produce a change of heart with this pretty darling.*

"You just do that, Jonah Sommer. I'll look for you," she concluded, giving his hand a final squeeze before quickly departing.

Jonah was stunned. *What had she said—she'd look for me?* He lay down again, a big smile on his face. *Well,* he thought, *some say absence makes a woman's heart grow fonder. Look you up, Miss Tennie? You can count on it.*

CHAPTER NINE

New Philadelphia

Eva lifted the hair on the back of her neck to take advantage of a light breeze, fluffing it out. "I love sharing days like this with you, Viola. Yet, Frank's story today has really taken us on an emotional ride of highs and lows."

"His brother really took a shine to that green-eyed gal," Viola commented. "Ah, to be young again and pursued by a handsome and brave fellow. That really would set my toes to tingling."

Eva laughed. "You talk like an old woman, sister dear. You've had your days of pursuit and young love. Were you always in love with Jimmy from the first time you met him?"

"There certainly was a strong attraction between us, which grew into deep love. Even so, dear sister, we're not heading west in a wagon and having the adventures of our lives in strange new lands. We're more settled now, as folks say."

"Frank's stories are so exciting, yet I do wonder. How much do you think that he's embroidering them, trying to impress me? You know, the gullible eastern woman fawning over the latest exploits of an adventurous western man, just like you read in the dime novels."

"What a question you ask. Surely, you can see that he's in love with you."

Eva was startled by her sister. "Pshaw, what could you possibly base that notion on?"

"I *read* his thoughts very clearly. Try opening your eyes and looking deeper, beyond the words. Then, you'll see what I mean."

"That's foolishness. Now, can I finish, or are you going to keep cackling like a hen for the rest of the day?" Seeing a nod, she continued reading.

Fort Laramie

As his brother walked into the infirmary, Jonah said in frustration, "I can't wait to scratch under the bandages and to get out in the sun again." He noticed that there was an older man standing behind Frank.

Frank laughed. "Sounds like good signs that you're recovering."

"Young man," the other man interjected, stepping forward, "we ain't been properly introduced yet. I'm Lemuel Spurgeon, but everyone calls me Lem. I'm originally out of Ohio and parts east, and most recently, the goldfields of California."

"Glad to meet you, Lem," Jonah replied.

"The prospector shook his hand and continued, "You surely saved my life the other day, and I'm mighty obliged and in your debt."

Jonah felt embarrassed. "No more than you'd do for me."

"Dadgum it, I mean what I say, son. I worked my fingers to the bone in the goldfields, and I got lucky and hit a right sizable pocket of dust and nuggets. You not only saved me, but you saved my poke. A couple more times under the water and I'd surely have died, or told them blasted scoundrels where I hid my gold. I want you to have this," he said, placing a leather pouch on the bed.

"That's mighty generous of you, Lem, but . . ."

"No buts about it. Take it, it's yours," the older man said. "I figure there's about three hundred dollars of gold dust in the pouch. That's my reward to you for saving my life and my valuables."

Openmouthed, Frank stared at the pouch.

"I don't know what to say, Lem," Jonah replied. "That's a high sum of gold. You sure this is what you want to do?"

"Yep," the old prospector replied, as he dug out his tobacco fixings. "As you can tell, I value my life."

Changing the topic, Jonah asked, "What's the California gold country like?"

Licking the end of his hand-rolled cigarette, the prospector lit it, grinned, and pulled up a chair to sit down. "Boys," he said in a spirited voice, "it's like nothing you've even dreamed about. Why a fellow last year found a single nugget that went nigh onto fourteen pounds, right there on a hill above Carson Creek, south of Stockton. You have any idea what that lump of rock was worth?"

"I don't," Jonah, answered honestly.

"Melted down, it fetched over two thousand dollars."

"Over two thousand dollars!" Frank repeated in amazement. "Why, that's a fortune for nearly a lifetime of work. And in one rock, you say?"

"Yep," the crusty, old prospector replied, with a chuckle.

With a dubious look, Frank said, "Ah, you're funning us, aren't you, Lem? You're just telling big stories to a couple of farm boys from Missouri. Ain't that right?"

Facing the two men, Lem Spurgeon's smile faded. "Looki here, I'm telling you the way it is. When a miner gives his word, it's as true as the day is long. Same when he spits in his hand and shakes, except then, his word is his bond. And I'm telling you what I know and the things I've seen."

Jonah laughed. "Well, don't go getting lathered up, Mr. Spurgeon. He was just asking because we've never been there. Are miners regularly finding nuggets that big in California?"

"No, not that size," Lem replied, "but finding smaller ones and glitter occurs often enough that gold fever has everyone in its grip."

"How do you go about finding dust and nuggets? Jonah asked. "Do you just turn over a rock and pick them up?"

"Most times, it's a hell of a lot more difficult," Lem replied. "More likely, you stake yourself a claim along some stream, and either with a pan or sluice box, you wash river gravel. It takes water to do that sort of mining, and that'll begin again this fall, when the rainy season starts."

"What's a sluice box?" Frank asked.

New Philadelphia

With the sun past its zenith, the two women remained in the shade, seated on the riverbank beneath a shade tree.

"This is such a long letter," Eva commented. "Are you sure that I'm not boring you, Viola?"

"No such thing, sister dear. Don't you dare stop! I just have to know what happens next to your wild man and his brother."

"All right. I'll finish reading this letter, then we had better pack up and leave."

"Lem was quite a storyteller, always talking about life in the gold-mining towns. He told us that some camps sprang up fast, like wild flowers after a rain shower, and became a city of tents overnight. He spoke about men striking it rich, and those who lost their fortune, maybe for a second and third time, at gambling halls and bawdy houses that follow gold miners, like bees after honey. I'm sure my eyes were wide with wonder. I had never heard of evil men preying on good folks and ladies of questionable ways.

As Lem talked, I saw the keen interest on Jonah's face, particularly when the old prospector began describing the antics of store merchants who supplied the miners. The older man referred to them as swindlers. He told us they charged triple for most everyday goods, and there were times when he saw prices rise five-fold in a single day, particularly when news of a gold discovery spread like wildfire through a mining camp.

My brother kept asking more questions, and Lem cited examples of men paying twenty dollars for a small bag of coffee that costs eight bits in most places. The old prospector said it cost forty dollars for a barrel of flax and one hundred dollars for a sack of sugar.

Then, Lem told us about 'Missouri cows,' and Jonah seemed to forget about his itch . . ."

CHAPTER TEN

Fort Laramie

At the hospital, Jonah listened to the old prospector's descriptions, and his mind raced with excitement.

"And that ain't all," Lem continued. "A fellow came through our camp with ten head of 'Missouri cows' for sale, and the miners went loco."

"What exactly is a Missouri cow?" Frank inquired.

"Damnation!" Lem retorted in annoyance. "What the hell do you think? They're exactly what the name says, animals bred in Missouri and herded two thousand miles over the mountains to the goldfields. Those miners bid up the price just to get a taste of back-home beef, paying as much as three hundred dollars for a single animal. I ain't ever seen anything like it."

Frank interjected, "We saw cows selling for twenty-five dollars each back in Independence."

"And biscuit flour," Lem continued, "I've seen store-keepers charge over eighty dollars a barrel."

"It's two dollars for a hundred weight back home," Frank countered.

"See what I'm telling you. Some of them fellows are making money faster than my Aunt Tootsie can wring a chicken's neck for a Sunday supper. So, let that be a lesson for you boys. There's more than one way to strike it rich in the gold country. Digging, mining, or sluicing streambeds are the hardest, most blister-causing, backache-numbing, and mindless ways of doing it."

Silently, Jonah listened to Lem's tales. In the back of his mind, an idea was forming.

"What's the most dangerous thing that you heard about on the trail to California," Frank asked.

Scratching his grizzled beard, the old miner pushed aside his hat and leaned back in the chair. "Well, it weren't Indians or accidents. No siree, I reckon it's the tales about the 'golden showers' that's the most blood-curdling. I fortunately never experienced it myself, but the talk about the sickness was on people's minds because it sneaks up on you and does you in, almost before you know it."

"What in blue-blazes is it?"

"Don't rightly know," Lem replied. "Folks get sick, sudden-like. They have the runs so bad till nothing is left inside them, but still it keeps on. Finally, they're plumb wrung out. I guess that's where the name comes from. They just seem to shrivel up and die. I heard tales of whole families being felled by the illness on the same day. Other stories tell about departed folks left alongside the trail, with some still resting in their beds."

"Heavens, that sounds horrific," Frank said. "It's a downright chilling way to meet your maker."

"Amen," Jonah chimed in.

The day after his release from the hospital, Jonah found Lem and asked, "Do you think that you'll ever go back to the goldfields?"

"I've definitely got the itch again, but I've got a deep pouch of dust, and I'm thinking that I'd best take myself off to St. Louie and have a grand old time," the prospector replied. "You know, I'll get myself cleaned up and buy me some fancy new clothes. Could be, I'll also get me one of them walking sticks, and, of course, a fine-looking woman, preferably a redhead, to hold on my arm."

"What would you say if I told you that I did the sums, and there really is a way to fatten your deep pouch, and you wouldn't have to pan streams again?"

"Sure, I know what you're going to say. Go back to the diggings and find myself another strike, or perhaps you'll tell me some far-fetched scheme that you've hatched up."

"No, it's nothing like that. I mean a sensible way to increase your fortune by, say, four times what it is at this moment," Jonah answered.

"Now, exactly how do I go about doing that," Lem asked. "You know, I've already dealt with all those two-tailed possum-fellows and gaudy-dressed, painted females in California. You're not trying to cook up a crazy scheme to get the rest of my gold, are you, young fellow?"

"No, of course not," Jonah replied, with a laugh. "But, before we talk more, Frank and I have to become your partners. Will you agree on that arrangement?"

"Partners in what? And how much of a stake do you boys have in this? What in tarnation are you jabbering about, boy? I see your gums flapping, but nothing you're saying has any gist."

"The idea is ours, for starters. Second, we'll put up half of the gold dust that you generously gave me the other day. Lastly, we'll do most of the work. But, our partnership has to be fifty percent for you and fifty for the two of us."

"Look, I don't know what in the hell you're thinking. Might be that your stay in the army's hospital has put you off your head a wee bit."

Ignoring Lem's comment, Jonah asked again, "Are we agreed?"

The older man dug out his makings and lit up before answering. "And you say this venture has something to do with California?"

"That's right."

Hesitantly, the gray-haired man said, "All right, I'll agree to your terms. Now, what in the name of Jehoshaphat is this weird scheme of yours?"

"Is that your word?"

"I said it, didn't I?" Lem affirmed, spitting into his hand and shaking Jonah's. "You know, son, a fencepost is generally more forthcoming than you are. Now, say it plain, so even a simple man like me can understand."

"All right, walk with me to the other side of the parade ground," Jonah replied.

As they went along, Frank joined them. "Where are you fellows going?"

"We're off to look at a pile of money," his brother replied.

A knowing look crossed Frank's face. "You mean your idea to get us all rich?"

"Yep, Lem has agreed to go in with us on a fifty-fifty basis."

"Well, I reckon, but I still don't understand what this is all about," Lem added.

Continuing, they stopped at the edge of the castoff pile.

"There it is, Lem," Jonah said, waving his arm expansively to the acres of goods. "That's piles of money, just waiting to be made."

Lem looked at the discards and then back at Jonah with a quizzical expression. "Boy, you really are a bit touched.

I see nothing here except them unwanted stuff. What, exactly, is this highfalutin' idea of yours?"

"You told us your tales about the high prices in mining camps," Jonah answered. "You're looking at furniture, crockery, equipment, tools, and all manner of other thinga-mabobs that we can sell in California to miners who have struck gold. What you're looking at is a rich strike for the three of us, a deep pocket, as you call it"

"You mean we're going to haul this stuff over a thousand miles to the goldfields in California?" Lem asked. "And how do you propose that we do that?"

"Why, it's simple, we'll buy ourselves wagons and mules, hire some men, and follow your route back to California."

Slowly, a smile broke out on Lem's face. "And I'm guessing that it's my poke, which will provide the money for all those things?"

"Plus our dust that we put in this venture," Jonah replied.

Craftily, Lem asked, "What stops me from doing all the things you said, and just cutting you two young fellows out of the deal?"

Jonah feigned a look of hurt and shock before replying. "Because you've been telling us that your word is your bond, and we spit and shook hands on our partnership. Besides, you'll need some strong backs for this job. And, you'll need folks to make sure you're not cheated at the mining camps. And those jobs are for Frank and me."

Lem broke out in a big, toothy grin. "You know, that's a mighty fine idea you have, Jonah. Let's go see what it'd cost for wagons and mules."

Jonah and the other two were shocked at the trading post's sky-high prices, yet he rationalized that they were six hundred miles west of Independence and over five hundred east of Fort Hall.

A wagon and team cost the outrageous sum of two hundred dollars, and they decided on two. They hired two privates, Alex and Gene, who were mustering out of the army and were itching to try their hands at panning for California gold.

The five men began picking through the "money pile," as they called the castoffs. Soon, they had sorted a fair quantity into separate piles of farming equipment, furniture, cookery—including stoves, pots, and dishes—and stacks of odds and ends.

"Now, Mr. Spurgeon, you being experienced in the ways of gold mining camps, which of these will fetch the highest prices in the diggings?" Jonah asked. "The ones you select will be the items that we take west."

The old prospector studied the sorted piles of discards and walked around them several times before speaking. "Once a miner gets beyond necessities like whiskey, food, and women, in that order, mind you, and he still has a deep pouch of glitter, he'll likely want creature comforts like these beds, stoves, soft chairs, and the like. I'm also thinking that we should pay the outrageous price here and take two-dozen kegs of whiskey with us. I've tried the trading post red-eye, and it ain't half-bad, compared to the watered-down swill that they sell in mining town saloons. And besides, those casks will cover the cost of this little expedition, because we can charge even more outrageous prices, selling it in the camps."

"So," Jonah began, "what you're saying, Lem, is that the things you pointed out are the only items we take? Some of these are mighty heavy, and we'd have to fetch really high prices to make it worth our while."

"Looki here, young man, you asked for my opinion, and I said my piece," the old prospector replied. "As we're not hauling any pretty ladies of the night, best we concentrate on the things I mentioned, plus the whiskey will be our hole card. But when it comes to these discards, we'll take only the best."

It took another week to sort through the items, pack the wagons, and sew the canvas coverings. Lem was particularly keen that the wagons were not overloaded, and he insisted on six draft mules for each team.

"The territory we're going to cover is rugged, and the mountains are some of the tallest that you'll ever see. We should buy another team, so we can rotate the animals. And one more thing, we also need to acquire several big, empty barrels to take with us."

Confused, Frank asked, "For heaven's sake, why haul the extra weight?"

"You mark my words," the crusty prospector replied, "the trail ahead is going to be dry and desert-like, with few watering holes and long stretches between. And even when you find water, it might be tainted with alkali. We've sixteen mules, five horses, and five men, and all are going to get mighty thirsty out there. We'll fill the barrels with water before we cross the really barren lands."

Fresh from the morning dew on a bright day in early June, Jonah, astride his horse, said the magical words that he had heard so often from Captain Fudge, "Wagons, ho!"

CHAPTER ELEVEN

New Philadelphia

"So, Viola, that's Frank's tale about leaving Fort Laramie for California," Eva said, beginning to pack up the remains of their picnic basket.

"Glory be, Ev, these adventures are truly amazing," Viola replied. "We have to leave now, but I can hardly wait until you read me another letter. Just imagine what a huge pile of stuff that must have been. And let's take pity on all those poor souls who had to leave their prized possessions behind."

As they walked home, they were light-spirited, chattering like young girls. Eva walked her sister home and then turned down the block to her father's house. As she opened the door, she vowed to write another letter to Frank before bedtime.

"Ev, is that you?" her father called. "Come into the study, please. I want to talk to you."

A feeling of dread came over her as she walked into the room.

"Have you been out with Will?"

"No, Viola and I went on a picnic down by the river."

"Oh, then you've already set a date with Will? When is the big day?"

A flush of anger touched her face, as she replied, "No, we haven't . . . I mean, I haven't agreed to a date, yet."

"And why in God's green earth are you dragging your feet?" Isaac asked, his voice tinged with annoyance.

"Because I'm not ready to commit to Will, or any man in New Philadelphia," she replied, feeling a storm of emotion overtake her.

"Ev, do we have to go over the same ground every time we talk? You're a mature, grown woman, but you're still acting like a muddle-headed schoolgirl. How many times do I have to point out that you're not getting any younger?"

"I've said my piece, and little will be gained by repeating it."

"That isn't good enough. Clear your head, and start thinking straight, young lady. I expect you to get on with planning your future. And I'm telling you right here and now that I expect you to set a date by the Independence Day picnic. Have I made myself perfectly clear?" he roared.

Eva, flushed with anger, managed to throw him a sweet smile. Leaving, she walked to her room with tears glistening in her eyes, seething inside.

In her state of frustration, she sat at her small desk, took a deep breath, and began to write her letter.

May 5, 1888

Dear Frank,

I reread your letter today and, yes, I do hope you'll be able to send me a picture. And yes, again, I have thought about a journey to see more of this big country. It's not easy to pick up and leave on a lark. I do understand that everyone needs someone, but I just haven't found that fellow yet.

There is a local man I've known for years who keeps coming around. He asked me to marry him months ago, but I keep putting him off. He's upstanding, yet I have difficulty considering him as a suitor. My father insists that I marry soon, and he is worried that I'll end up being an old maid. He mentions my two sisters, who are married, and he thinks that I'm way overdue to follow them down the church aisle.

I can't seem to make him understand that there are things I want to do with my life, like exploring brave new worlds and discovering magnificent sights. Here I am, carrying on about my everyday routine, while you have a life filled with adventure and excitement all the time.

Tell me about your fishing river, as you call it. Does it have a name? Is it big and wide? Is there more than one river in your area that you fish? What kind of fish do you catch? How about the Indians, do they fish, too?

You told me about the new cabin. When do you expect to complete it? Is it located very far from your present one? Is it located near a river or high on a hill?

And how in the world did your birthplace come to be called Six Bulls? Someone must have had magnificent animals for the area to take that name.

Here I am, asking question after question, but I am curious.

I'll close this short note for now. Please know that you are never far from my thoughts.

Your dearest friend,
Eva

———————————

Three weeks later, a man hurried into the library, looking around as though lost.

"Good morning, sir, may I help you?" Eva asked.

"Yes, I'm looking for Miss Eva Mae Helms," he responded. "I have a telegram for her."

"That's me," she replied in astonishment, as a momentary thrill ran through her. She had never received a telegram before.

"It came all the way from Washington Territory, way over by the Pacific Ocean. Here it is, ma'am. Please, sign on the line to show that it was delivered."

"Thank you."

"G'day to you," he said, tipping his hat to her.

With trembling hands, she unfolded the yellow paper. She read the hand-written message once, blanched, and read it again.

She could not have been more stunned, yet a lightening bolt of excitement shot through her. Eagerly, she reread the short message, then again.

THE WESTERN UNION TELEGRAPH COMPANY
—— INCORPORATED ——

Date	May 31, 1888
Rec.	June 2 1888
Del.	June 2, 1888

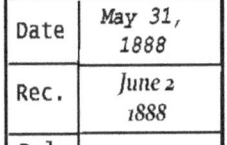

Dearest Eva. Marry me. Details in letter.

I love you. Frank.

Oh, my God, she thought. *Can this really be happening?* Still reeling, she thought, *I have another marriage proposal. And from a man I've never met. There are so many things I don't know about him. What if he's a drunkard or curses frequently. How deep is his voice? Does he laugh often? Will his touch be gentle or rough? What will father say? Forget him,* she counseled herself, *what am I going to say?*

As her mind leaped ahead, she sat down hard behind her desk, suddenly weak in the knees. *Could I really leave all that I've ever known and travel to the wilds of Washington Territory? What would Mother say? What would Viola and my other sisters think? How in the world would I ever explain it to Will?*

These and many other thoughts raced through her head. Quite suddenly, her mood was light-hearted, and she felt giddy. *Can I really up and leave, and travel alone for over two thousand miles?* Pausing to consider the matter, an exhilarating mixture of joy and wonder swept over Eva, and her mind cleared. *You're darn right I could do it,* she determined. *That challenge would not stop me!*

Two weeks later, Frank's letter arrived. Eva was in a daze during the intervening days. Friends at work found her distracted. Even her father's lectures sloughed off her, as she merely smiled at him and went to another room without arguing, leaving him perplexed.

Viola seemed particularly mystified at her sister's sudden preoccupation. Not only that, but Eva abruptly stopped reading Frank's letters to her. She inquired, yet her sister simply refused to be drawn into a long conversation.

Instead, she usually said something insignificant like, "We'll talk about it soon."

Through it all, Eva was cheerful and went about her job and life, inwardly excited and anxiously awaiting the arrival of Frank's letter.

On the day it was delivered, she nearly ran into the book stacks to read in private. Tearing the envelope open, her hands shook. Trying to calm herself, she unfolded the pages.

May 31, 1888

My dearest Eva,

I received your last letter and immediately sent the telegram. Don't marry anyone in New Philadelphia. Instead, marry me. You and I, we will carve out new lives in this vast frontier wilderness where we can be proud to raise the young ones that become a part of our family. Yes, the land is raw and untamed, but that makes it more exciting to be here at the beginning, as this territory is surely growing. It is rich in timber, mining, fishing and a life that has largely passed by many eastern states. And on top of it all, the land is beautiful with its abundance of trees, tall mountains, and water—lakes, rivers, the inland sea, and, farther west, the deep blue ocean.

For these many months, I've come to bless the days when your letter awaits me. My heart aches, as I read them over and over. Your last one nearly tore me apart and made me face the fact that I've come to rely on your strength and, in my own clumsy way, I'm trying to say that I love you and want you to be my wife. I want us to be together for the rest of our lives.

I pray my proposal doesn't upset you or turn you away from me. How I will wait with eagerness for your next letter.

Eva stopped and found that she had been holding her breath. Once again, she was taken by his outpouring of love and his tender offer.

When she closed her eyes, she tried to imagine the marvelous sights that he described and tried to picture him doing things about the cabin.

Stirring herself, she read on.

Think of it, Eva. Traveling west will be a grand adventure for you. You have nothing to fear, as you'll be with other travelers. Please know that I will pay the seventy-five dollars for your journey. My gold-mining activities keep me well supplied with money, and that's the least of my worries. I'm not sure how you get to Chicago from New Philadelphia, but local inquiries will provide the answer. The train from Chicago travels across the plains and over the Rocky Mountains to the Great Salt Lake and then on to San Francisco. Regrettably, the direct rail line to Seattle is only now being constructed, and a line through my community of Wallace is also in process. From San Francisco, I suggest you take the mail packet boat bound for Seattle. Lastly, a small steamer sails twice a week to Cadyville, which some are beginning to call by the Indian name of Snohomish. I will be at the dock when you arrive, my dearest. I know the trip can sound confusing and, perhaps, daunting, yet, my love, just think of the adventures you'll have.

I don't mean to assume anything, and please do not think me forward. The above is simply to explain how your journey would progress.

You also asked about my log house, and here is a brief update. It should be finished in the next month. I'm waiting for the rain to let up. Then, I can add the roof, which will be clad in split cedar shingles, the same method used by the local Indians. It keeps the interior much drier and lasts for years. My Indian friends have been very helpful in advising me and showing me how to water seal beneath the wood. Additionally, I have been busy splitting shingles and have quite a pile. Fortunately, I had a good-sized cedar tree nearby, and its fragrance has provided a bonus of spicy scent during the construction.

The cabin has a great room for cooking and eating. It also will serve as the parlor to entertain friends. There are two bedrooms, and a mudroom to shake off the rain. Out front, there is a porch with a plank floor and roof. It'll be a wonderful place to sit and watch the last rays from the sun shimmering on the Wallace River below. I hope with all my heart that it becomes a home for both of us.

This note is shorter than most, as the steamer will soon be leaving for Seattle, and I don't want to miss it. I pray that you have feelings for me. If yours are not yet as strong as mine are, please don't let it turn you away *from me and our writing. If your letters stop, I know part of me will die.*

Imagine, Eva, what exciting times you will have, traveling and seeing some of the marvels of this huge country. You'll ride the train across the plains and the tall, spiny mountains of the nation, then sail the Pacific Ocean to Seattle. We will fish in my beautiful river named Wallace, hike the forest-covered mountains, and journey on the big rivers.

Come, Eva, come to Washington Territory. Come to me. Please answer as soon as possible. I eagerly await your reply.

All my love,

Frank

As she neatly folded the letter and began placing it in the envelope, a small photograph tumbled out. Staring at her was a handsome man, with a trimmed beard, dark hair and eyes, and with wide shoulders. *My, he's tall and strongly built,* she reflected, *and very manly.* A nerve of excitement shot through her. *He must be a good cook, for he certainly doesn't look like he's underfed. Yes, the fellow staring back at me is a mighty fine looking man.*

CHAPTER TWELVE

Rain from a summer storm drummed against the windows of the library, as Eva sat at the table, lost in her thoughts. All her co-workers had left for the day, while she had lingered, telling them that she wanted to catch up on the latest book offerings.

In truth, she wanted to reread Frank's last letter in privacy, which was increasingly difficult at home, with her father storming about every time he saw her. She delayed answering his letter, yet she repeatedly turned the proposal over in her mind. At times, the idea of traveling and marrying Frank gave her a giddy feeling and, strangely, like she was being unshackled. Other times, she dreaded the thought of leaving everything and everyone she knew. Such moments lasted until she slipped his picture from her secret wooden chest and stared at it, trying to imagine the sights and excitement of covering thousands of miles by herself and then living in the deep forest with this resourceful man.

She settled herself in an overstuffed chair near the window and began to write.

July 5, 1888

Dearest Frank,

I waited to receive your letter before answering the telegram. Both of your messages surprised me and leave me breathless. You have made me an astonishing proposal, and one that I value very much. Even so, I find myself torn by conflicting emotions. Everything I have ever known is here in New Philadelphia. Still, I am drawn to the lands out West, and I excitedly think about traveling over the long distance to Washington. I, too, have come to value our relationship, and I so look forward to receiving your letters.

I hope you can understand and will permit me time to think on the matter. I expect to respond more completely in the coming months.

I will not accept another man's marriage proposal without writing to you first. I give you my word, and I will keep it. I know this is not an answer, but please let my promise be sufficient until I can clear my head and think straight.

I'll keep this letter brief to respond more quickly.

Yours very affectionately,
Eva

That evening, Eva sat in her room, brushing her hair. There was a discreet knock on her door, and Viola stuck her head in.

"May I come in, Ev?"

"Of course."

Her sister sat on the bed and stared at her. "You know, you missed father's deadline to set a wedding date by Independence Day."

"So?"

"Well, what comes next?"

Almost casually, Eva replied, "I have a lot on my mind these days. Frank Sommer sent me a telegram a few weeks ago, and today I received another letter from him."

Amazed, Viola asked, "Really? He sent you a *telegram?*"

"Yes, and in his message, he proposed to me."

Viola's mouth silently opened and closed twice, until she finally stammered, incredulously, "He proposed what?"

"You heard me. Besides Will, Frank Sommer has asked me to come to Washington Territory and marry him."

"Oh, my heaven's above!"

"He also asks me to come as soon as possible and wants to send money to pay for the trip."

Still bewildered, Viola stared at her sister, Again she asked, "He proposed by *telegram?* Why, I've never heard of anyone doing such a thing. Why, you know that's . . . that's special . . . really special." Seeming to gather herself, she questioned, "And you're mulling it over?"

"Absolutely."

Viola snapped, "Ev, you can't just up and skedaddle, leaving your family and your job and Will and me and everyone you've known all your life. Or, can you?"

"I'm not sure, but I'm thinking about it."

"Well, what else did he say in the letter?"

"He told me that he loves me, and he provided some of the travel details. I'd take the train from Chicago, west to Sacramento. Afterwards, my trip continues by sailing to Seattle and then to Cadyville. Why, do you know that it costs more than seventy-five dollars to get there?"

Her sister was momentarily lost in her own thoughts, her face tinged with excitement and a look of wonder. "Lordy, all this news is almost more than I can take at one sitting. The trip would be such an adventure and then the life after . . .," she trailed off, momentarily lost in her thoughts. Shaking off her reverie, she asked, in quick succession, "Do you love him? Are your feelings strong enough to undertake such a step? Could your really leave everything you've known all your life?"

"I've given it a lot of thought. I'm drawn to him, of that I'm sure."

"What about father? And what about Will?"

"What about them? I haven't made a choice, so there's nothing to tell, at least not yet."

"Let me ask one more time, do you love him?"

"I'm not quite sure. If it is, it'll not be a choice I make, because love is a gift that comes to a woman who is blessed with it."

Viola examined her curiously and then grinned.

Watching her sister, Eva could tell that she was swept away with the prospect of such an adventurous trip.

"And you'd marry the man? That's what he's proposing, isn't it, marriage, not merely someone to warm his bum on a cold night?"

She nodded, raising a cynical eyebrow.

"That would be utterly beyond belief. And, he'd pay for it?"

Dreamily, Eva answered, "Yes, it would be unbelievable."

Crossing her arms and tilting her head, Viola mused, "My, he must love you very much. I've said it before, and

I'll say it again, this man sounds very lonesome out there in the woods, with only raccoons and bears for company. Well, that's beside the point. How can you possibly consider his proposal? You've never seen him, much less met him. Why, you don't even have an image in your head of what he looks like?"

"Well, I have seen him, because he sent me a picture." Teasingly, she inquired, "Would you like to see it?"

"Are you kidding me? Stampeding horses won't stop me," Viola replied, taking the picture from her sister's hand. She studied it at length. "He's very handsome, with his dark hair and beard. And, my land, he certainly does have broad shoulders, doesn't he?"

"Aye, he does."

"Do you think it's possible to fall in love with a picture, sister dear?"

"What do you mean?"

"Well, you obviously aren't put off by his proposal or his looks. Even so, I don't see you skipping about, or running to catch the next train west. Therefore, the question hangs in the air, waiting for your answer. Do you think it's possible to fall in love with a picture and letters from a man you haven't met, with whom you've never exchanged a single word, nor even heard him laugh? Maybe he snores like a bull or drinks like a fish or chews tobacco or spits on the floor or, my goodness, the many things you don't know until you're actually with him."

"Oh, Viola, you are a tease. I'm drawn to him and to his strength. He knows what he wants out of life, and he's reached out and grabbed it. But, truth be told, you are right, I'm not hopping around like an excited schoolgirl. I can tell you this. When I first read his proposal, my heart beat wildly and my blood raced, and both are doing exactly the same at this very moment."

Weeks later, Eva sat in her room, holding a recent letter from Frank. Rain showers tapped upon the window, and she marveled at the beauty of a red rose just beyond the windowpane. *I feel like I'm a rose, too, and my inner sap rises every time a new letter comes from Frank. How will I know if it's true love? Heavens, is there some magical way to know? Perhaps, I'm fooling myself and leading him along. All I can say is that, once again, my heart is beating rapidly, and my pulse is racing, just holding his unopened letter.*

With trembling hands, she slit open the envelope and began reading.

July 26, 1888

Eva, my dear love,

Your short note arrived several days ago, and I have been wondering how to respond. Certainly, take your time to sort your thoughts. I just hope that my proposal wasn't too great of a surprise, or that it somehow ruins our chances for happiness. Please don't stop writing to me. Both of us will lead only one life, and I hope that we can be together for all eternity.

Ever since we began writing, your letters have helped me come to life. I gladly paddle my dugout canoe down the river in eager anticipation, hoping the next one from you is waiting for me at the Mr. Cady's trading store. When there is none, I feel low, as though all my breath has been knocked from me.

That is how I feel right now, but I realize my marriage proposal must have come as a shock to you. I, too, was torn when you said you had a proposal from another. I feel like we are at an awkward point, and I pray that this will pass quickly. Well, permit me to set this aside and say a few words on other matters.

The cabin exterior is complete. I am working on the fireplace, and, next, I plan to lay down the plank floor. The local mercantile has a cook stove that burns either wood or coal. I have in mind buying it and using the fireplace only for warmth. What do you think? Is an indoor stove a good idea, in your experience?

Some Indian braves came downriver last week, and I traded furs for smoked salmon. I think these fish are the finest tasting in the world. Last fall, I caught six, and the largest one must have weighed at least forty pounds.

By the way, the name Six Bulls comes from the first white man to live in southwest Missouri. When he was young, he feared that civilization was settling over the country too fast, so he left Tennessee for the Missouri frontier and lived with the Indians for nearly twenty years. When he returned east, he told many tales about the frontier lands. Among his stories, he kept talking about six bulls, until someone asked him to explain. It turns out his English had deteriorated to the point of pronouncing the word "boils" (you know, springs that feed rivers and streams) as "bulls." I know you're laughing, but it is God's truth. To this day, the area continues with the name, Six Bulls.

To tell you the truth, I am really not sure what else to say. Perhaps, I can get back to relaying more about Jonah and my passage west. It may help us get beyond this point in our lives. Is that all right with you? I hope you're nodding your head yes. Well, here goes.

I'll pick up the story after we left Fort Laramie and traveled toward Fort Hall in Idaho Territory, and the point where the trail to California splits from the one going to Oregon.

Along the way, we came across an unbelievable series of events. Jonah was leading and I rode drag, when we came to a frontier mail drop. Do you know what that is? Well, here is the answer . . .

CHAPTER THIRTEEN

Idaho Territory

Jonah led the small party down a narrow gulch and onto a broad plain. More than a month had passed since the five men departed from Fort Laramie. Lem drove the lead wagon, and Gene handled the other one. Alex looked to the extra mules, strung in a line at the rear. It was hot, and the land was covered in a haze of heat.

In the distance, through the shimmering waves of heat, Jonah observed a strange sight and pointed it out. There stood a stack of multi-colored rocks of various sizes, nearly four feet tall.

"That's a frontier mail drop," Lem called, from his seat on the wagon.

"Hell, it's probably the 'parting of the ways,'" Gene shouted from his perch on the second wagon.

Riding up beside his brother, Frank, added, "It's an interesting way to leave messages for others. I can see where it would be uplifting for folks coming along this way."

Jonah dismounted and lifted the top rock. Below, there was a gaggle of messages, written on odd scraps of paper. "The top one says, 'you have arrived at the parting of the ways,'" he told the others.

Everyone cheered. It was another milestone on their long overland journey to California.

Gene let out a chuckle as the group gathered around to peer at the fork in the trail, with wagon ruts running in two different directions. Taking off his hat and wiping his brow, he said, "Keep going south, and you come to Fort Bridger in about a week's time; and from there, the Mormon Trail leads to the Great Salt Lake. On the other hand, you can travel north from Bridger to reach Fort Hall in another two weeks. Now, taking this other fork westward, you're on the Sublette Cutoff, which saves eight or nine days of travel, despite few water holes and steep mountain grades. At its end, a traveler has another week to reach Fort Hall. So, what's it to be, gents, three weeks or two? By the way, just beyond the fort, the trail splits again. The west fork is the route to Oregon, and the one headed southwest delivers you to California."

Jonah was half listening, as he scanned other messages. Most notes were addressed to friends or relatives. "Say, here's one that's really interesting," he said, suddenly very excited. "It's dated last fall and says that another big gold strike has been discovered in California, north of a place called Mount Shasta Butte, but on the flats." He stopped, puzzling how to pronounce the tricky name. "It's called E-rek-a or U-ra-ka. Maybe it's Y-rek-a. Any of you fellows ever hear of such a place with this strange sounding name? Frank, take a look at this note and see if you can say it differently?"

"I can't do any better than you, brother. It must be Y-re-ka."

"Lem, you ever heard of this gold-mining area?"

"Nope, I spent my time prospecting in the hills east of Sacramento."

"I don't exactly know the place your saying," Gene replied. "Yet, I do know something about the area. Alex and I traveled to California with the third expedition of Lieutenant John Fremont. While camped on the Sacramento River, I was part of a troop that was sent north to explore. We followed the large river up to its source, which is the biggest doggone mountain I've ever seen, called Shasta Butte. I reckon it's the tallest mountain in the whole U.S. of A. Traveling toward it, you can see it from any direction for days, as the top is always covered with snow and ice."

"So, like the note says, Yreka must be north of the mountain, but I reckon it's still in California," Jonah reasoned. "I wonder if this would be a good place to peddle our trading merchandise." Jonah looked at Lem. "What say you, partner?"

"I have no idea where this mining camp is. But listen up, I do know two things. Finding color attracts droves of miners to an area, like flees scurrying to a fresh patch of hair on a hound dog. And second, prospectors will be itching to buy things with their newly found wealth. I've seen it happen many times. This place sounds exactly like it has the right bunch of customers for our wagonloads."

"Let's try it and take this cutoff." Frank added. "It should save us over a week, and besides, we filled our empty barrels with water days ago, so we shouldn't get thirsty. Gene, after we get to the end of this part of the trail, any ideas on how we get to the northwest side of Mount Shasta?"

"I think so. On the expedition, we came across a fellow by the name of Jessie Applegate, who had already homesteaded in southern Oregon. He was leading a group of riders, and they were establishing a new trail to Oregon, one that allows settlers to enter Oregon from the south-east, rather than the treacherous route along the Columbia River. And, they named the route the Applegate Trail.

"Once we get clear of this shortcut and Fort Hall, the California Trail follows the Humboldt River for nearly four hundred miles, until it dumps into a basin. The Applegate Trail hives off from there, going through lava buttes and desert wastelands of northeastern California. Before I left soldiering, I traced the latest army maps of the western territories. These days, there are several variations of the Applegate Trail. One of these travels to the north face of Mount Shasta Butte."

"Well, boys, are we agreed that Yreka is our destination?" Jonah asked. Seeing the nods, he said, "It's decided. Off we go, and we'll turn west and take the cutoff. Wagons, ho!"

The land became unending lines of mountains running north to south, covered with sage and scrub grass. The men were hot and tired, while the days dragged on, and trail dust ate into their souls.

They double-harnessed the mule teams to haul each wagon up the steepest slopes, but going downhill was hellish. Besides the double teams, each rear wheel was lashed in place with a large log to create a skid. The added drag slowed the wagon's momentum on the slopes. Riders on both sides held ropes tied to the back end, to steady and control the rear. When one wagon successfully reached the bottom, the team of mules was driven back up the hill to handle the next. It was hard and dangerous work, yet it was the only safe way to control the heavy wagons on the steep grades.

Along the cutoff route, they passed the skeletal remains of a number of wagons that had been abandoned over the years.

Seeing still another, Frank exclaimed, "Tarnation, folks must not know what they're getting into when they take this cutoff. Otherwise, they'd have made better preparations for water. These relics are downright eerie."

Lem added, "Folks overload their wagons, then they come to the steep mountain trails, and their animals get worn-out. Mix that together with a shortage of water, and you have a recipe for death."

"Just like Captain Fudge and Shep predicted on our wagon train," Jonah said to Frank.

The route took them through several narrow, rock-strewn gorges. The men again found themselves in another one.

Jonah exited and looked down into a gulch paralleling the trail. Suddenly, he reined in. "Frank, come look at this."

Unbelievably, a large herd of cattle was spread out in the broad bottom of the boulder-strewn *arroyo,* feeding on scrub grass. To one side, they saw the tents of the drovers, with thin lines of smoke rising upward in straight lines from several campfires.

"Why, there must be nigh onto a thousand head in that draw," Frank exclaimed.

"I reckon you're right," Jonah agreed.

Driving the lead wagon, Lem reined in and stared down at the astonishing site. "That looks like trouble to me."

Jonah looked at him with a quizzical expression. "What kind of trouble? It looks peaceful enough."

Lem simply pointed toward the turkey buzzards circling above an area, farther up the gulch. "Take a look with your spyglass. What're them things stacked up that look like cordwood?" he asked.

Lifting his glass, Jonah gasped. "My God, those aren't logs, they're dead bodies! There must be ten or more. By all that's holy, what's happened here?" He handed the glass to Frank.

Below them, a man came out of a makeshift tent and stumbled, as he walked unsteadily toward a campfire. Turning, he saw the group on the ridge and waved his hat. Cupping his hands, he shouted, "Hello, we need help."

Another man appeared beside him, and looked up. He began waving his arms enthusiastically, until he lost his footing and slipped, tumbling down a small slope. With great effort, he rose to his knees and then collapsed.

The first man shouted again, "We got men dying all around us in this canyon, and we have no medicine."

Frank shouted, "What ails you folks?"

"Fact is, we don't rightly know what's got us down. Those of us remaining don't have the strength to bury our friends after dragging them up the draw. Please, we need help!"

"Reckon it's that sickness we talked about weeks ago, the 'golden showers,'" Lem quietly said to his companions, who were clustered and standing along the rim.

Another man emerged, this time from the largest canvas tent.

"Howdy," he shouted. "Me name is James Henry Sparks, and we're from Arkansas Territory. Our party is the California Emigrating Company, and I'm the mayor of Forth Smith. We're driving the cattle west to sell in the mining camps."

"I'm going down there," Jonah said, turning to look at his party.

"Better not, son," Lem cautioned.

"We have to do something. These folks need help."

"Don't be a damn fool," Gene cautioned. "If their ailment is what Lem and I are figuring, we're most likely watching the walking dead moving about down there. I've seen and heard of similar things happening, and it's called by various names like the golden showers, but the one that really describes it the best is the 'silent killer.'"

"You fellows stay up here on the trail," Jonah said. "I'm going down to see if there's a way that we can help. Can any of you advise me on how I best approach them?"

"Boy, I'm a telling you, you're likely risking death if you mingle with them," Gene cautioned.

"Do any of you have a suggestion?" Jonah repeated.

"Sure, let's be on our way and move down the trail," Alex replied. "You have to be loco to go near that camp."

"We can't do that," Jonah snapped. "Any *other* thoughts?"

Lem took off his hat and wiped his forehead. Looking at the young man, he cautioned, "Don't get close to no one. From what I've heard, the ailment might be spread by just touching the sick or their gear. And, for God's sake, don't eat or drink anything."

Alex pointed toward the circling turkey buzzards. "Look at that pile of departed men. The Grim Reaper is waiting for more fools who wander close. Anyone touching and burying them is probably asking for the same fate."

"What are you saying?" Frank asked. "You don't mean that they shouldn't have a decent Christian burial, do you?"

"Yes, what do you mean?" Jonah added.

"Like Lem says, don't touch anything," Gene responded. "That way, you may stay alive. Say it anyway you like, you're risking your life, son, and most likely ours, too."

Jonah paused before speaking. "Look, I'm no braver than the rest of you. These are folks like us, no different, except now they need help. How do we know that we weren't placed here for the very purpose of providing comfort?"

Sarcastically, Alex added, "It's another Sermon on the Mount, only this time it's not spoken by a prophet, but rather by our youthful leader who, truth be known, ain't saintly."

"God save us from fools," Gene whispered.

Turning quickly toward the former army men, Jonah snapped, "I know you don't much like being here. And that goes for me, too. If you fellows got something to say, then spit it out."

Gene stared at the ground. "Sorry, those are my views."

Jonah looked at each one before speaking. "No one else is on the trail within at least a day's ride. We're obliged to deal with this ourselves."

"Jonah," Lem added calmly, "your sense of duty and brotherly charity has overcome your common sense."

Frank looked at the others. "Brother," he finally said, "I'm unsure of your wisdom on this matter. Yet, I'll follow your lead. I also feel obliged to help these folks, if we can."

"I'm much obliged to you, little brother." Turning to the others, Jonah asked, "Well? We're all partners in the scheme to sell merchandise to make ourselves rich. You have every right to protect yourselves. I'll understand if you feel you must go on without me."

Alex stared at the ground, and Gene's face was drawn and pale.

Lem finally summed up the group's thoughts. "Do your best, Jonah, but stay your distance. Carelessly dying on a wilderness trail ain't part of our plans. Even so, you're right. The Lord may have called us here as Good Samaritans. Let's hope God is with you."

Mounting his horse, Jonah slowly made his way to the bottom of the rock-strewn canyon. At the bottom, he caught the whiff of rank odors, and he held his bandana to his nose. *You stubborn, dumb jackass,* he thought. *Why in tarnation are you here? If Gene's right, the ones still living are only the walking dead. My partners must think that I'm acting like a wee youngster at Sunday school class, filled with thoughts of sugarplum charity. Am I throwing away my life by simply being mulish?*

Approaching, he saw tents and crude, lean-to covers, created with odd-shaped branches and scrub brush, draped with canvas and weighted down with stones. Under the shelters, he saw a few men lying on grass pallets, too weak to stand. The camp's listlessness was unusual, considering that a stranger was riding into their midst. In fact, it was alarming, as though the reaper was secretly lurking beneath each of the makeshift shelters—and likely, he was.

A woman rounded a tent and greeted him with a nod. Her drawn face was smudged with dirt, and the dress she wore had once been blue and white gingham, but it had become frayed. She was a fine figure of a woman, and he reckoned that she was about ten years older than he was. Her red hair had tumbled down on one side of her face, and exposure to the sun had heightened her freckles.

"G'day to you, ma'am, I'm Jonah Sommer, and those fellows up on the trail and I are on our way to the California goldfields. What's happened here?"

"Nice of ye to ask. My name is Lisa Annie Sparks," she said, drawing her shawl closer over her shoulders. "That's me husband who called out to ye." She spoke with a lilting brogue from the old country, as she brushed aside a strand of hair from her freckled face.

He saw James Sparks approach with uneven steps, leaning on his rifle. The man appeared to be considerably older than his wife was, and he was having difficulty standing. Dressed oddly, with a cutaway green coat over a once-white shirt, his black trousers showed the wear of long trail rides.

"It's God's will that ye folks came along," the mayor said, also speaking in a lilting voice.

"Howdy." Jonah replied, remaining in the saddle. Wary, he asked, "What's happened here, and how is it that you haven't buried your dead?"

"It's the strangest thing we have ever seen," the mayor replied. "We passed the 'parting of the ways' ten days ago and came over the cutoff. After driving our herd through the mountain passes, we veered off into this canyon and alighted here to rest.

"We found water for the cattle back yonder, and six days ago, my men started getting sick and dying. Each came down with fearful bouts of the runs and nothing helped. Some showed signs of the illness in the morning and were gone to meet their Maker by midday. They died so fast that me and me men can't keep up with burying the departed. We've lost eleven good lads. And now, we're too worn-out to do any more burying. It isn't very Christian-like. Nevertheless, all we can do is remove the departed from camp."

"How many of you are left?" Jonah asked.

"Well, Lisa Annie came down with the sickness, yet pulled through. Besides me, there are fifteen other men. Some are showing signs."

"Good Lord," Jonah replied. "A man in my party has seen ailments like this before, and he tells me not to touch anything down here. We have no doctor and only a short supply of herbs and medicines. What do you need?" He noticed that it was an effort for Mr. Sparks to remain standing.

"I wish to God that I knew the answer. My Lisa Annie seemed to take quinine well, however, we ran out two days ago. Do ye have any ye can spare? I'll pay ye whatever ye ask."

"Yes, we can spare some."

Jonah sat his horse, thinking. *I can't expose my partners to this. Even so, I can't ride off and just leave these folks.* Taking off his hat and moping his brow, another thought struck him. *By God, I don't want to come down with this curse. If all it takes is being near the center of death in this God-forsaken gulch, then I might already be on the path of becoming one of the walking dead. Still, we have to do something.* "I'll ride up to the ridge and talk with my men. Might be they'll have more thoughts on what to do next. How many cows are in your herd?"

"We started out last year with near a thousand head in Fort Smith. I reckon that we've lost about a hundred on the trail—you know, broken legs, snake bites, and the like. All the perils one expects to encounter on the trail."

"Lost any while you've been camped here?"

"Nary a one."

"Are any showing signs of sickness?"

"I don't think so, but I've been too weak to ride and check today."

Something puzzled Jonah and prompted him to ask, "That's a long way for a cattle drive, with what, two dozen men, covering a journey over thousands of miles?"

"Aye, we started with sixty-eight men, besides the wife and me. We arrived in the Salt Lake area last winter. Many of me lads had the gold itch bad and left us to go on to the diggings. This spring, the pace of driving the herd was too slow for some of the others and off they went, bound for California. On the trip, two accidentally died when a trail gave way. All told, that makes thirteen who have gone to meet our Maker, so far. Good lads, they were."

The appalling losses astounded Jonah, as he backed his horse. "I'll be back soon." Digging his heels into his horse's ribs, he made the steep climb to the top of the ridge.

"So, what's happened down there?" Frank asked.

Jonah noticed that his partners kept a reasonable distance from him, despite their curiosity. "They need quinine. It seems to have helped the woman, as she survived the illness. Their leader says they've lost eleven men here in the canyon, and another fifteen are in camp, and some show signs of the illness." Jonah saw the looks of concern.

"I figured that they'd be happy to see you or anyone," Alex said warily. "Where are they headed with those cows?"

"They're on their way to the California gold diggings, and Mr. Sparks, their leader, says they have some nine hundred head of cattle. He also told me that none of the stock has died while they've been camped here."

Gene wasn't much for talking, yet he had no trouble expressing himself on this matter. "It ain't no skin off any of our butts what happens to them folks. Let's be on our way. These folks show every sign of having run across bad water and being afflicted with the golden showers. If I'm right, the damn sickness may already be blowing our way. I say again, let's get."

"That's not the Christian way," Alex responded.

"I kind of lean with Gene," Lem added.

Jonah studied the men for a moment before continuing. "Look, I ain't leaving folks who are in such need, and that's final! Let me tell you my plan."

Jonah's men used a mule team to lower a heavy barrel of water on a rope sling. None of the cowpunchers below offered to help Jonah at the bottom, which was fine with him, as he wanted to keep his distance.

The mayor, his wife, and the others sat outside the largest tent, watching and waiting.

Keeping his distance, Jonah dismounted and squatted in front of the survivors. "One of the men in our party is a former army man, and he's seen an illness like this before. He thinks you've come across bad water, and that is what's ailing you folks. It doesn't seem to harm livestock, but to people, it's deadly.

"We aren't doctors, but we do have some suggestions. From this point on, use only the water in the barrel over there. To make double sure, boil it first. Our man figures that all the clothes and bedding that you've been using may spread the sickness. His suggestion is that you burn all the possessions from those who died. You can keep any clothes you have, but first boil them. Then, wash yourselves with water from the barrel. It also seems like the right idea to drink lots of our water. These suggestions make sense to you, Mr. Sparks?"

"Heavens, we'll try anything. Ain't that right, men?" he asked, looking around.

"Perhaps Mrs. Sparks can help tend to the sick," Jonah continued, "as she's survived this outbreak. I have the quinine you asked for, ma'am."

"I'm greatly obliged."

There was an air of listlessness among the survivors, which contributed to the awkward silence.

Anxious to return to the canyon rim, Jonah said, "Mayor Sparks, the scrub grass in this ravine is nearly gone. Is there anything you want us to do?"

The mayor seemed baffled by the question.

Instead, Lisa Annie answered, "We have to find new grazing for the cattle, and soon. Would ye please ask yer men to scout ahead to find more feed and water for them?"

"Yes, we can do that."

Her husband was looking in the direction of the bodies. "Ye men will surely help us bury me dead comrades, won't ye?"

"I'm sorry, sir. I can't ask them to take that risk." Hesitating, he continued, "To be sure that they aren't a continuing source of the illness, I suggest that they be burned, along with their personal belongings."

Immediately, shocked expressions appeared on their faces.

"Ye want us to do what?" Mayor Sparks asked, suddenly alarmed. He was shaking, as he stood, leaning on his wife. "Be ye daft, young man? Is there not a Christian bone in yer body, when ye make such outrageous proposals for me dearly departed lads?"

Looking at the others, he saw disbelief on their faces. He turned back to the mayor. The man's face was flushed, and his short speech seemed to sap his energy. Suddenly, he sat down hard on the ground.

"That's the most disgraceful and unchristian thing I've ever heard," Lisa Annie stormed. "Why, just the thought brings all kinds of images to me mind. It'd be like Lucifer's inferno in hell for those poor departed souls."

"Believe me, I understand your shock. I was raised in a family of believers and have similar views. However, this isn't a normal situation, and you've already lost many lives to the sickness. None of us is practiced in this matter, as I said, but there's one thing we do know, fire cleanses. Recall the Bible verse, when Isaiah said, 'The Lord will cleanse the bloodstains of Jerusalem by fire.' I'm not keen on the thought of burning the dead, but right now, you need to think about living. It comes down to a really simple question—do you want a better chance to live?"

"And not give them a proper burial," the older man stormed, again.

Jonah stood. "I can't force any of you to take my suggestions, but my men and I are leaving unless you follow all my directions." He stopped, letting his words sink in. "I'm sorry to be so blunt, but those are my terms. The choice is yours."

The group looked around, and many shook their heads.

Dejectedly, Mayor Sparks finally answered. "Well, we're in no position to argue. Despite our distaste for the task, we'll do it, but they need the proper words said over them."

"All right," Jonah said, relieved that they agreed to the precautions. "My group will camp on the ridge tonight. Follow my instructions carefully. Everything, including clothing, food, utensils, and anything else that's been touched by the departed must be burned. Wash yourself and your clothes with the new water and don't forget to boil it. In the supplies over there, you'll find a jug of coal oil. Spread it over the whole lot and put a flame to it, after you've said your words."

───────◆━━━━━◆───────

Jonah was eager to depart from the "valley of death," as Lem and Gene called it. The next morning, Frank and Alex found new grazing several miles farther along the trail, and the herd was moved to a grassy area with a spring. They and most of the drovers stayed with the animals and the wagons.

Mrs. Sparks tended the sick. Two more died, while the rest seemed to grow stronger. The mayor, however, was in a bad way. Late in the afternoon, Lisa Annie waved to Jonah on the ridge. "Please come down, Jonah. Me husband wishes to talk with ye."

At the bottom of the ravine, she waited.

"Is the illness easing up?" he asked.

Uneasily, she replied, "Perhaps. But after so many days, it's best to wait and see."

Cautious about getting too near and anxious to leave the canyon hellhole, he followed her and stopped some ten feet from the Spark's big tent. Sitting on his heels, he nodded to the mayor.

"Thank ye for coming, Jonah," the man said. He sat on a campstool near the fire. "It must be God's divine hand that brought you to us. Ye and yer men have given us hope, but I fear I'll not be taking up the trail again."

Jonah heard the mayor's wife quietly crying off to the side. A blanket of sorrow seemed to have descended on the camp, and he felt it keenly.

"I've two last requests to make," the mayor began, in a shaky voice. "We're still days from Fort Hall in Idaho Territory, and me wife needs to be safely escorted to California. Will you please see her to yer destination?"

As a tear ran down his face, Jonah nodded. "Of course, sir. We're bound for a gold camp called Yreka in Northern California, and I'll see that she gets there."

"And what's to become of the herd, young man?"

"I'm not sure how to answer your question, sir."

"Think on it. Each of them cows cost me less than twenty dollars. In a mining camp, they'll likely fetch fifty or sixty dollars apiece, maybe more, because they were bred in Missouri and Arkansas. Why, young man, it'll be like manna from back home. That was the whole idea behind driving such a large herd over the backbone of this country."

"Sir, I'm completely open to any thoughts you have."

"Will ye and yer men help me men see the herd through?"

"We'll try."

"Then, we're agreed. I'll write out a bill of sale giving ye and yer men half of the herd in consideration for seeing me wife safely over the trail. She will own the rest and take care of the wages of the men still able to ride. Does that sound fair to ye?"

"What? My Lord, sir, that's overly generous. You're talking about giving away thousands of dollars."

"Aye, but they'll not be of great use where I'm off to next. What does matter to me is that me wife is safe. I've had a fine, long life, and she deserves the same. I once thought that I could provide it for her, but . . ." His voice trailed off as his head dropped. Seeming to summon his remaining strength, he looked up at Jonah again. "Ye must promise to see me Lisa Annie to civilization, even if it's that God-awful-sounding place ye call Yreka. With the sale of the cattle, it'll tide her over. Those are me terms," the older man rasped. "Are we agreed?" The strain of talking was evident.

"Yes, sir."

"I believe ye, young man."

"I also have a concern, sir. With the few men left, the big herd will be difficult to handle over the rough trail that lies ahead. I'm told the land becomes more barren and rocky, and that water is scarce."

Totally exhausted, the man whispered, "Do the best ye can, me boy. It's all any of us can ask of ourselves."

———◆———◆———

The next day, the remaining cattlemen and Mrs. Sparks were on the trail to the new camp. Behind them, plumes of black smoke rose high into the sky from the burning funeral pyre.

Mrs. Sparks was sobbing, and most of the men brushed away tears.

Jonah suspected that all of them shared a conscience of guilt. Though thankful for having been spared, each realized they were lucky, while others were taken. And likely, this would be their memory forever of the canyon of death.

Before leaving, Lem dug out paint from the supply wagon to create a notice for other travelers on a large flat rock. He drew two human skulls to mark the canyon of death and added the word, "WARNING." He referred to it as another type of frontier mail drop.

Making a sign of the cross, Jonah said, "God rest your souls, boys." He turned his horse west, as black, oily smoke billowed into the sky behind him.

CHAPTER FOURTEEN

New Philadelphia

Eva hurried into her room, shaking inside. When she was sure no one else was in the hall, she closed the door and placed a chair against it. She wanted privacy this evening.

Worry lines creased her forehead. *How do I know what's really on Frank's mind? I can't be sure, can I? People may say anything in a letter. It's not like sitting across from him, hearing his voice, and seeing the way he carries himself. How would I know if he was just telling me tall tales about his adventures to catch my interest? Is he another womanizer, like that Stephan-fellow?*

Today started well for me, she recalled. *Well, that is, until the Friends of the Library meeting in the late afternoon.*

Eva found a chair at the large gathering. Despite the threatening weather, the meeting room was nearly full, and the air hummed with many conversations, as women found their seats and greeted friends.

Arranging her skirt and settling, she mused, *the room sounds like the chattering of magpies that sit in father's trees every summer, squawking at everyone as they walk by.*

Chairwoman Hagadorn rapped her gavel, and the library's entry hall, fitted with rows of chairs, slowly quieted. She stood before them, beaming, with her eyeglasses in place, the attached golden chains dangling from the stems before gracefully curving around her neck. "Friends of the library and my dear acquaintances, we have a full list of items this afternoon, so may we begin. I wish to remind you about the upcoming performance by the Cleveland Symphony Orchestra, and its presentation of music by Paganini and Rossini. This performance is its first outside of the big city. I'm sure that it will be a splendid and enjoyable evening for all who attend. And, I might add, it's quite a feather for us that they choose New Philadelphia."

Eva had purchased advance tickets, and she was taking Viola to the performance for her birthday. Both were looking forward to the night out.

Mrs. Hagadorn called on several members, who provided updates on association activities. Then, she took questions from the floor on each matter. The woman's agenda seemed endless, as the meeting dragged on.

Eva noticed increased fidgeting about the room and observed more than one lady casting a covetous look at the table set against the library wall, filled with pastries. *I wonder how far attendance would fall, if sweets and coffee were not on hand after the meeting.*

Next on the agenda was the *Washington Effort*, a project Mrs. Hagadorn enthusiastically supported. Smiling broadly, she continued, "I'm happy to report that more than half of our members are participating in this compassionate project, writing to the lonely, godforsaken men in Washington Territory. Many of you have told me about the glowing responses you've received from those poor souls. It has been uplifting and most satisfying, has it not?" she asked, rhetorically. "It's a wonderful way to pass an afternoon from time to time," she noted.

Well, I suppose so, Eva thought, *unless, of course, you're raising a passel of youngsters; then, there are other duties, like keeping house, washing and mending clothes, wiping drippy noses, and cooking—breakfast, noon, and evening— and you're still expected to have enough vigor to handle amorous advances in bed.*

Mrs. Hagadorn continued, "Ladies, please rise and each of you can tell us about your personal experience on this most gratifying, commendable, and compassionate letter-writing campaign."

Standing, one after another told how rewarding it was, and of the gratitude heaped on them by the forlorn men who received their letters.

Then, Chairwoman Hagadorn called on Agnes, sitting in the fourth row.

Eva knew her, as they had exchanged pleasantries several times, when the young woman visited the library on her day off from work. She lived alone in a boarding house located a few blocks off the town's main road.

Shyly, Agnes stood and, in a low voice, addressed the audience. "I did want to share my gratifying experience with you. That is, until this past week." She stopped and, looking down, twisted the handkerchief in her hands.

The ever-beaming smile on Mrs. Hagadorn's face drooped a little, as she urged, "Well, go on, dear."

"I had no idea that such a strong friendship was possible, using only the fine mail service we have today. Stephan, that's my pen pal, and I have been writing for over eight months. He has regaled me with stories about his adventurous travels west and life on the wild frontier. I have learned so much from him, like the times he and others fish the rivers for large fish called salmon. He also reports that most Indians are friendly, and his fears in roaming the woods center on bears and blow-down trees. When he's not logging giant evergreen trees, he works the streams, and he tells me that he has a deep pouch of gold dust and nuggets to reward his efforts."

Eva shifted uneasily in her seat, recalling similar words in Frank's letters.

Uneasily, Agnes continued, "Our friendship has grown, and I look forward to Stephan's letters. Then, his last one arrived." She dropped her eyes, the handkerchief twisted beyond recognition. Half-heartedly, she continued, tears welling up in her eyes, "His letters have always been so interesting and happy, yet this time all that changed. His words and manner were uncouth and demanding. He insists that I travel west immediately, so, as he put it, 'we can merrily sail through life, knowing that we will always be in each other's arms, warmed by our lovemaking.'"

To Eva, the words sounded somewhat puffed up and coarse, yet there was flair to the phrase. She heard tittering from a few of the ladies in the audience.

Slowly standing, an old woman reminded them, "I told you no good can come from writing letters to wild men in the West."

Another began, "It's not very romantic, yet it has a certain, rough charm that is . . ."

Belligerently, the woman seated next to her snapped, "What possesses a man to assume such liberties?"

"Shame on him!" still another said heatedly.

There is a certain amount of righteous smugness drifting about in this room, Eva thought. *However, Agnes makes no mention of any marriage proposal from her Stephan. H'mm.*

Still standing, the young woman replied, "I wish his words ended there."

Immediately, the room quieted. There was a state of hushed expectancy and speculation on whether salacious details were about to be revealed.

"He wrote that he would pay for my travel fare to ease my mind and satisfy any burden for money, while allowing me to come without delay." Again, Agnes halted, her cheeks damp with tears.

Mrs. Hagadorn took a step back, and seemed painfully aware that she had no idea what was coming next.

"Then, my pen pal wrote the following." Agnes paused to take a letter from her pocket and unfolded it.

A charge of energy gripped the room, as more than a few ladies edged forward in their chairs.

In a voice filled with emotion, the young woman read, *"When you arrive, the bliss of fiery love will descend upon us, as I lift your veils, and you admit me to your wondrous triangle of love."*

Audible gasps came from the crowd. Numerous comments swept the room, coming from all quarters in quick succession.

"Scandalous!"

"Brash and outrageous, that's what he is."

"Vulgar and disgusting," another said, loudly.

"Your man's gone straight from pen pal to pent-up lust."

"It's unacceptable behavior in this day and age."

"Oh, you poor woman," a woman across the room called out.

At the back of the room, someone uttered, "In my opinion, what your pen pal really wants, deary, is to snuggle with your warm derriere on cold nights."

Planting her cane firmly on the floor and rising to stand yet again, the elderly woman sternly wagged her finger in everyone's general direction and, with a quiver to her voice, uttered, "I issued my stern warnings to this group at the beginning of this program, but no, you modern young ones wouldn't heed the advice of an experienced woman like me."

Poor Agnes, Eva concluded, *there's slender chance of her living this down in the community, even though she is only the bearer of the news. Interestingly, a hint of eager excitement seems to be in the air. I'll wager that some of these hypocrites will need an extra measure of lye soap to wash their bloomers tonight.* She smiled at the thought, but it quickly faded. *What about Frank and me, and what does he expect? He, too, has offered to pay for my travel. I do want to trust him. Yet, could I be in the same shoes as this young woman, simply a toy for sordid gratification, to be used until the day that I'm discarded? That's not my Frank. Or, is it? Have I badly misjudged him and his intentions and what about . . .*

Agnes' next harsh words interrupted her thoughts. "Friends, consider that he's asking me to travel far from home and be his . . . be his . . ." Already mortified, she could not finish the thought. Then, she added, "He thinks I can be persuaded by uncouth words and delivered by post."

A loudly whispered voice said, "Right on that score, Agnes, and he thinks you're the woman he can beckon at any time to satisfy his lewd appetites, when his urge arises."

Chairwoman Hagadorn was aghast at the turn of events. Her face was pale, and her eyeglasses hung from the gold chain about her neck. Rapping her gavel harshly, she demanded, "Ladies, please retain some decorum. After all, we are patrons of the library, and we must conduct ourselves . . ."

Interrupting, someone in the back of the room insisted, "Why are any of you surprised that the carnal instincts of wild men are displayed, especially if they are living in a godforsaken land like Washington?"

"It is man's beastly instinct," still another woman said, sitting in front of Eva. 'Lustful craving lays just beneath the skin of every man, not just our pen pals."

"This letter-writing business is no more than a bawdy house by mail."

"That's it! I'm through sending letters to Washington."

"I warned of such goings on, didn't I?" the very old lady repeated, still again.

"Ladies, members of the association, we must show more restraint when making remarks. And please, for the sake of our organization, let's all show a greater degree of modesty," Chairwoman Hagadorn pleaded, as she banged her gavel several times.

The woman seated in the front row stood and waited for everyone's attention. "I was against this undertaking from the start, and I mean to say my piece. It's perfectly obvious that the fellow wants to corrupt one of our members. And you can bet that the same notion is on the minds of all those lonesome pen pals. We never should have taken on such a risky task for our association. If word of this gets out, that we're playing cat and mouse and *femme fatale* games with wild strangers, the integrity of our entire library program will be jeopardized." Mockingly, she added, "It's clear that he wants something sweet all right, but it isn't candy he's looking for. Some in this room call it a compassionate project. Uh-huh, in a pigsty's eye, it is!"

A strong murmur of agreement swept through the crowded room.

Mrs. Hagadorn sat down hard in her chairwoman seat, perplexed and humiliated.

Egged on by the many comments, Agnes remained standing, her cheeks inflamed with righteous indignation and, surprisingly, her posture had become ramrod straight. "Here, I thought my writing to him helped still his loneliness, while giving me the satisfaction of comforting someone far removed from civilized lands. Now, Stephan asks that I live in shame, outside the sanctity of both family and church." Nearly shouting with righteous anger, she raged, "Never! I shan't be bought like a hand muff from one of those new mail-order catalogues."

Applause filled the room, as the meeting ended in disarray.

The poor girl, Eva thought, as everyone quickly split into groups to chew on issues of morality, which Agnes had deliciously presented, while nibbling on sweet tartlets from the side table.

Chairwoman Hagadorn remained seated, an expression of exhaustion on her face. Her arms hung limply over the sides of the chair, the gavel dangling from one hand.

———◆————————◆———

The comments from the meeting roiled Eva, as she sat in her room at home that evening. The longer she thought, the more vexed she became. Too agitated to sit, she began pacing. *Is that what men in the West think of us eastern women who write to them? Do they really think that we can be bought by paying for the price of a rail ticket, and that we'll simply jump into their beds, panting with desperate eagerness?*

Suddenly stopping, she said to the empty room, "Well, we'll see about that. I'm going to write to Frank this very minute and make things perfectly clear, so we have a proper understanding."

August 1, 1888

Frank,

Let me be plain. If and when I decide to travel west, it will be at a time of my choosing. Should this occur, I alone will pay for my fare, and there will be no need for you to think otherwise. I am a modern woman, living in the year of our Lord, 1888, and I am fully capable of making my own decisions.

Further, when I marry, it will be to someone who is loving, caring, and will not take me for granted. Nor will I marry a man who treats women as pawns. I shall never be anyone's femme de corrupteur. Please be advised that these are my strongly held views.

Sincerely,

Eva

CHAPTER FIFTEEN

With tears in her eyes and a catch in her throat, Eva began reading the letter, as her sister lounged on her bed with a pillow.

"September 18, 1888

Dearest Eva,

By golly, I am not sure what prompted your last letter. I have been scratching my head, wondering what I could have said that so offended you.

I am sorry, but nothing comes to mind. Despite this, I apologize for having upset you and ask you to accept my sincere regrets.

I hope we can make amends. Please keep in mind that my marriage proposal is genuine and heartfelt. Yes, I consider myself a loving person and one who could never imagine taking you for granted. Can we put aside whatever triggered your last message?

I had a letter from Jonah a while back. He worked in the Jacksonville gold mines for several years and then bought 145 acres in the back hills east of town, along the Applegate River. By the way, he never did hook up with that green-eyed gal, Tennie, from the wagon train. His first wife, Hanna, died some years ago. He remarried and has five children. My brother even donated several acres for a community cemetery, just as our family did back in Missouri. He says everyone refers to it as the Sommer Cemetery.

The new cabin is nearly complete. The doors and window coverings have yet to be fitted, and I am working on finishing the caulking between the timbers, as well as building new furniture. I have also ordered the cook stove that I mentioned earlier.

I am going upriver to a fall festival later this month at the invitation from some friends, which is held at the Indian encampment. It should be interesting, and smoked salmon will be served. I wish you were here, so we could go together. I understand there will be some contests, as well as events for the younger folks. I am honored to be invited.

I'll close for now and hope that I have explained myself to your satisfaction. Please believe that I love you and want to be your husband and your lifelong companion. I have no hidden motives, no mysteries, nothing else, just my love. And finally, I am a caring man. I have faith that we can treasure and respect one another through eternity.

All my love,

Frank

Additive: Don't think me a dunce or too back woodsy, but what in the world is a femme de corrupteur?"

"Good Lord in heaven above, Viola, I said terrible things in my last note to Frank," Eva cried, tears rolling down her cheeks. "But, the young woman at the library meeting was so shocked about her pen pal's words that it upset me terribly. And then, the reaction from the women at the meeting was disturbing. Honestly, some of the comments were simply scathing, and I got caught up in it. It stirred my worst fears and doubts. So, I wrote the letter without really thinking, and I said words I shouldn't have." She buried her head in her hands, sobbing. "What am I going to do?"

"Things happen, dear, and none of us is perfect."

"How do I make amends?"

"Have you made up your mind between Will and Frank?"

"Will is nice and all, but I'm torn."

"Do you want to end the relationship with Frank? It's certainly easy enough. Just stop answering his letters."

"Oh, no, Viola, I couldn't do that. I look forward to receiving them, hearing about the progress on his cabin, and his life in the forest. You and I, we've both enjoyed his tales of adventure. No, I'm not prepared to do that."

Viola cocked her head and fixed her with a sympathetic look, then smiled. "All right, I think this letter writing has been very good for you, and probably him, too. Get on with your life, dear. Write to him and explain that you just had a bad week. He'll understand."

"Do you think so?"

"Yep, I'm sure of it."

Eva nodded. "You're so wise and caring, Viola. I don't know how I could have managed to hold off Dad without your support. I'll send Frank a letter today."

"You'd also better recognize that you have feelings for this wild man. And they are deep ones, by my reckoning."

Wiping her eyes, she stared at her sister. Gradually, she smiled and nodded.

From another room, they heard their father. "Ev, are you in your room. I want to talk to you before you leave for work this morning."

"Ah, I know what's coming," Eva said.

"I think you're right."

"Well, I might as well get the daily barrage over with. Another letter arrived from Frank earlier this week. Would you like to hear what he has to say?"

"Indeed, I would."

"Wait for me."

———◆———

Eva walked back into her bedroom, flush with anger. "Well, Viola, I guess father's many lectures have finally penetrated. I can't tell you how distressing these talks have become. He thinks that he's helping, but the real effect is that he's pushing me away."

Sympathetically, her sister nodded. "I know, dear, and I feel for you."

Sighing, she asked, "Are you ready for the next reading? This was written only two days after the one I just read."

Lying comfortably on Eva's bed, Viola had a look of expectation on her face, as she waited to hear the latest from the "wild man."

Heaving another big sigh, Eva began.

"September 20, 1888

My Dearest Eva,

You have probably received my previous letter. I shortened it, as the packet steamer was sailing, and I wanted to respond to your unusual note. So, think of this as a continuation of my last dispatch.

You have not asked, but I thought I would relay the story of how I came to Washington. By the way, many folks here are talking that this territory will soon become a state in the union.

No one else died after we left the canyon of death, and we were all truly thankful for God's mercy.

After re-provisioning at Fort Hall, we followed the Humbolt River, through some of the wildest country that you can imagine. Over long stretches, we saw few trees and nothing grew taller than our cows. Yet, there were always distant mountains to be crossed. At one point, our route was filled with jagged stones. It got so that we dismounted and moved rocks so our teams and wagons could pass.

Nearing the eastern side of the snowcapped mountain called, Mount Shasta Butte, the land was rugged. As we were having breakfast one morning, a lone stranger approached the camp, coming out of the morning mist, there in the middle of the most untamed wilderness imaginable. The big stranger dismounted, and I saw Jonah shaking hands with him and then, to my utter amazement, they clasped each other and hugged. For the life of me, I could only wonder what was happening, until ..."

The Captain

CHAPTER SIXTEEN

Yreka, California

In the dead of night, Captain Renke Vogel remained hidden behind a large equipment shed, watching three men fugitively approaching the lantern-lit entrance to the Sourdough Wind gold mine. One stayed outside the ring of light as a lookout, while the others climbed over the gate and disappeared into the dark tunnel that had been dug into the side of the mountain. The only sound was the thundering noise of the stamping mill crushing rock, coming from down the hill. It was loud enough to be heard throughout most of the broad Yreka Valley, day and night.

The lookout outside the main entrance was barely distinguishable in the weak light.

Despite his age and large size, Renke Vogel was light on his feet, as he sneaked up on the guard from behind

and used the butt of his pistol to knock the man unconscious. Tying his legs and hands together, he made sure
that the thief would remain there until he returned.

Entering the mine, he lit a stick of kindling from an
overhead lantern. Extra headgear lamps hung on a rack,
and he took one and used the flame to ignite the small,
mirrored candle, then strapped it on his head. He continued into the tunnel, following the dim candle-lit path
before him. Nearly one hundred feet through the passage,
the harsh clamor from the stamping mill faded, as he came
to the edge of the main vertical shaft, which dropped sixty
feet straight down into bedrock. Below this level, four tun-
nels radiated from the mineshaft, following and tapping
into the rich gold ore veins that dipped into the bowels of
the earth. The seams varied in width from inches to several feet, as these wound through solid rock formations.

He carefully peered over the edge and saw a dim glow
coming from a newly dug tunnel two levels below. *Looks
like these gents know more about the Sourdough than is
good for them*, he thought. Pausing in the shadows, loose
pebbles from the edge dropped down the deep chasm and
into a pool of water at the bottom. The only other sound
was the rhythmic, sharp echo of a pick striking rock, coming from the tunnel below.

Using the weak light from his headlamp, Renke swung
his head to cast a beam of light on a worker's station
located near the shaft. Searching among the tools and supplies, he found a gunnysack. He slit two strips with his big
knife, tying one on each boot, to muffle his steps. He also
put several Lucifer sticks in his inside coat pocket.

When the winch in the shaft worked during the day, a
large iron bucket carried men, tools, and gold-bearing
rock between the tunnel levels of the shaft. The only other
way up or down was to climb the vertical wooden ladders
that were deeply affixed into the rock sides of the shaft.

Stepping slowly down the rungs, he arrived at the lowest level. Snuffing out his candle, he carefully followed the dim light coming from the other end. Rounding a bend in the crooked passageway, he stopped as he heard voices and the continuing sound of a pick at work.

"C'mon, T.R.," a man said, "put your back into it. I want to fill this last sack, so we can get above ground again. This soggy, dripping cave has me spooked. Another few shovel loads and I'm leaving."

Mockingly, the other said, "Wes, there ain't nary a soul nearby at this late hour, except for Trace up top. None, that is, if you don't count the ghosts of all the miners buried down here by cave-ins. And no one need fear them because they've gone to the big mine in the sky."

"Funning me, aren't you, T.R.? This hole in the ground reminds me of the graves I've dug at the town cemetery. Let's just finish and get."

Captain Vogel cautiously made his way along the side of the eight-foot wide passageway, guided by the light glinting off the rock sides ahead, yet he remained hidden by the unevenly excavated walls. He stopped behind several huge timber posts that held one end of the crossbeams supporting the heavy ceiling above. Bending down, he gathered a handful of small pebbles. With a flick of his wrist, he sent some flying along the tunnel floor toward the mineshaft.

"What was that?" Wes asked, lifting the lantern high to shine more light down the passageway.

Staring toward the dark entrance, T.R. replied, "Aw, it's just some loose stones falling down the main shaft. It happens all the time."

Renke tossed his last pebble in the same direction.

"There it is again," Wes said, nervously. "I'm satisfied with what we have in the sacks, and I'm leaving right now. You coming?"

"Oh, all right," the other man replied. "You're as antsy as an old pussy cat. Anyway, I reckon that we've got about as much in these gunny sacks, as we can haul up the ladders."

"You got that right. Tomorrow, we'll extract the gold after we smash and wash the rock in the stream south of town. Now, let's get."

"Evening, boys," Captain Renke said, in his deep, rich voice, which seemed to rumble off the walls. He moved to stand in the middle of the passageway. "I didn't know that we had a graveyard shift working tonight."

Startled and turning around quickly, square-jawed T.R. said, "Hell's fire and damnation, where'd you come from?"

His partner dropped his sack and turned with the pick clutched in his other hand. "How did you know we were here?" Wes asked, lifting the lantern from the floor.

Ignoring the question, Renke continued, "You boys know that it ain't fitting to steal from someone else's claim. You probably also know that it's a hanging offense in this mining camp. And that'll be just what you men will be doing come sunrise, dangling from a tall tree with a tight noose around your necks, along with your partner up top."

T.R. surveyed the captain. A thin smirk split his face, "You're a big fellow, but there's only one of you." Grabbing the lantern from his partner, he raised it higher. Then, with a wicked grin on his face, he continued, "Why, judging by the white hair that I see hanging below your hat, you're an old-timer, aren't you? You shouldn't be trying to scare us two fellows who are in our prime."

Wes let out a derisive laugh. "Where's your help, old man? Maybe you have a posse standing behind you. Or could be that it's waiting topside? How're you planning to stop two of us? Best you back off, grandpa. Go on home and sit yourself in a rocking chair to ease your aching bones."

"We'll see," Renke replied. "I work for Thorne Cort, who owns the Sourdough. He takes right badly to having his gold-bearing ore stolen."

"Who in the hell are you," Wes asked.

"I'm the enforcer hereabouts, and my name is Captain Renke Vogel." He could tell by the expressions on their faces that they had heard of him. "Best you step to one side and drop any weapons you're carrying. Be nice little boys," he taunted, "and do as I ask."

"Go straight to hell," T.R. replied.

"Now, now, let's don't have our tempers get the best of us. You'd best look around. You do know that you've been digging in the unsupported end of this tunnel?"

"You must be dense," Wes responded. "Of course, we know where we are."

"I'd be mighty careful, if I was you, because the support posts and crossbeams holding up the ceiling above your heads have yet to be set."

"What in hell are you chawing about, old-timer?" T.R. asked.

"Neither of you must be very experienced. Most miners know that an unsupported ceiling can give way at any instant. Some say that even a loud sneeze can cause a cave-in."

A sudden look of fear appeared on Wes's face. Quickly, he slung his pick with deadly intent, aiming it at the captain.

Nimbly stepping to one side, Renke was irritated. "Try that again, and you're dead men. You fellows have two choices. Give yourselves up, or die in this hole. What's it to be?"

"We'll die topside anyway, so no sense in prolonging this with useless talk," T.R. replied angrily. With a quick motion, he pulled a long knife from his boot.

Even faster, the captain drew his six-gun and fired twice. The deafening roars in the confined tunnel echoed and reverberated against the walls, hurting his ears.

Immediately, a dense cloud filled the chamber, and the thieves' lantern light dimmed to a hazy glow. After long moments of fearful waiting, the air began to clear, as dust and debris settled to the rocky floor.

"Ha!" T.R. said, grinning with relief. "That wasn't even close to being an interesting situation. Get thee gone and out of the way, old man."

Quick as a flash, an ear-splitting, thunderous roar filled the narrow passageway, as tons of rock and dirt crashed down, demolishing the end of the tunnel. With only an instant cry from one thief, both were buried beneath the rubble.

Ducking and turning toward the wall to avoid a dense blast of flying dirt and fragments, Renke hugged the wall, burying his face in the crook of his arm.

The raucous boom resonated with deafening intensity and then rapidly faded, as it moved at lightning-fast speed through the passageway, up the shaft, and out the entrance.

Coughing heavily, he finally reached inside his vest pocket for a Lucifer stick and struck it on the wall. With his headgear candle burning again, he cast its faint beam on the cave-in.

"Well, you boys saved yourselves from being hung, yet justice was done. But damnation, now this end of the tunnel will have to be dug out again.

"Have yourselves a nice sleep, boys. See you soon enough . . . probably in Hell."

CHAPTER SEVENTEEN

Thorne Cort sat at the rear of the Elk Horn Saloon, watching the crowd and the goings-on. He saw Captain Renke Vogel enter through the double-winged doors at the front. His enforcer was a big man, standing over six feet tall and broad across the shoulders. The mine owner noticed that the man's step was that of someone much younger, as he moved through the noisy, smoked-filled room.

How old is the captain? He must be in his fifties. Could be that he's turned sixty. Yet, the man's amazingly fit. He's always trimly dressed in black, from his broad-brimmed hat to his boots. In these gold diggings, his clothes contrast sharply with those of the miners, who usually wear grubby, mud-splattered boots, canvas pants, and faded wool shirts over long-john underwear.

The big man reminded him of someone who was always ready to accompany the town's hearse on its journey to Boot Hill. *I guess you can say he dresses for the job,* Thorne thought, with a chuckle, as a cruel look played over his face. *He also looks a bit haggard. Could be he's lost some weight.*

He detected the outline of a holstered pistol beneath the big man's black coat. *Probably has that long hunting knife on his other hip,* he speculated. He also noted that the sourdoughs gave way to the captain and that more than one pair of eyes warily followed him, as he walked toward the rear of the noisy room.

Vogel was on his payroll to do the nasty work of enforcing his orders. *Sure, the town council goes through the motions of adopting the rules,* Thorne thought, *but those men damn well do what I tell them. These sourdoughs would steal me blind, if they didn't respect and fear a man like the captain.*

Cort came to the Yreka area soon after gold was discovered. Previously, he kicked around the Sacramento River Delta area, using various shady schemes to enrich himself. When he arrived, work began immediately on building the Elk Horn. Then, he branched out into mine ownership. Rumors swirled in the camp that he had a hand in swindling the original owner out of the Sourdough Wind Mine.

Since that time, his operations rewarded him handsomely, but the heavy machinery was expensive. It was built in the East and came around the tip of South America, up the Pacific Ocean and Sacramento River, and was finally hauled over the mountains to Yreka. Each item was vital in the process of getting tons of gold-bearing rock from the bowels of the mine to the mint in San Francisco. None was greater or more expensive than his gigantic stamping mill.

From the main tunnel, mules hauled the rock in iron-wheeled carts to a hopper outside the entrance. There, the rock funneled to the five-stamp mill to be crushed. In the last step, the material flowed into large, rocking sluices, where water separated the heavier gold ore from the rock sediment.

Without water, the operation of the Sourdough Wind Mine in Greenhorn Canyon came to a complete standstill. During the rainy season, a wing dam on Humbug Creek accelerated the current, forcing water into a flume built of rough-sawn planks. Sloping downhill, the structure extended for miles and crossed many draws, *arroyos,* and canyons, supported by heavy, stout timbers. Cort's men replaced sections of the waterway each summer, as weather and the rapidly flowing water took their toll.

Sixty-five feet above the mine entrance, the water funneled down into cast-iron piping that progressively became narrower in diameter, accelerating its force. This provided the power for the main shaft winch, stamping mill, and the rocking, gold-separating sluices.

Cocking his head, Cort heard the sounds of the crusher over the din in the smoky, crowded saloon. *That heavy thumping is music to my ears, because it means ore is being crushed, with more gold for me.* He smiled, thinking about the dry months. *When that mill stops for maintenance, or in the off-season, the stillness is so absolute that everyone complains that it's too quiet to sleep.*

No settlement existed before gold was accidentally discovered by a passing traveler. The passerby noticed the glitter of golden flakes caught in grass roots dangling from the mouth of his grazing mule. Word of the gold discovery spread like a wildfire, setting off frenzied searches. Within six weeks, over two thousand miners worked the area. After six months, the number ballooned to five thousand. A city of tents sprang up overnight, largely replaced in the last two years by newly built, wooden structures. The town had grown to the point that it now contained many boarding houses, saloons, brothels, stores, blacksmith shops, saddler, stable, and other places of business serving the large mining town.

His "palace of pleasure," as Thorne liked to think of the Elk Horn, contained ten gaming tables, as miners crowded around their favorite. One featured the game "chuck-a-luck," where men tossed dice from an hourglass-shaped cage. "Twenty-one" and "lump o' gold" poker were two of the favored card games. More recently, a roulette wheel, shipped from Savannah, Georgia, was his latest addition. Arriving at the coastal harbor of Crescent City, it was hauled east over the mountains to Yreka. At odds of thirty-to-one, it was paying for itself especially fast.

In one corner, miners exchanged valuables for chits, which were good for anything that was offered in his pleasure palace. The exchanged items were later resold in the mercantile store across the street and, frequently, they were repurchased by the previous owners. Conveniently, Thorne also owned the store, yet another gold mine for him, where supplies, food, and equipment were typically marked up four or five hundred percent.

He told everyone that he sold his whiskey below cost to bring customers into his establishment. In truth, a glass of redeye, as the fiery liquor was called, was bloody expensive. Besides chits, the only other "currency" used in the saloon was gold dust. To pay for a glass of redeye with gold, a bartender stuck a wet finger into a miner's pouch of dust. The gold-encrusted finger was then swished clean in a water jug behind the bar that collected the valuable glitter at the bottom.

Plying their daily trade, the rooms for his working girls were at the top of the landing, and a steady stream of customers climbed the stairs. In its own way, this was another moneymaker for him. Every summer, he sent a wagon to the flatlands, seeking new faces for his upstairs bordello. He referred to the annual trip as stocking his corral.

One man worked the Elk Horn in the quieter, early-morning hours. After a boisterous night of carousing and gambling, he swept the sawdust-covered floors, saving the leavings in barrels. Later, the material was panned, which typically produced a few ounces of glittering gold that carelessly had fallen to the floor.

Truth is, this town is one gold mine after another for me, he thought. *And it's making me richer than I ever dreamed, and no one is going to stop it. That's why I have enforcers on my payroll, to assure everything continues to operate smoothly.*

As befitting a Northern California baron, his clothes were tailor-made in San Francisco. This evening, his long brown coat matched the trousers, highlighted by a tan-colored waistcoat, and complete with a gold watch and chain, strung from the one pocket to another, and passing through a vest buttonhole. A man in his early fifties, his eyes were dark beneath thick, shaggy eyebrows. His hair was the color of sand sprinkled with salt. Walking with a limp, the man used a cane, which lay on the table in front of him.

This walking stick was a treasured possession. He often told the story about having purchased it from a down-and-out man, claiming he had been a former Russian nobleman. One of the cane's beautiful features was the intricately shaped, solid-bronze handle, which housed a cleverly disguised lever. With a flick of his finger, a hidden trigger materialized, transforming the cane into a firearm, capable of killing a man at fifteen paces.

He reached for his tobacco fixings and began his fastidious and elaborate routine of creating a cigarette. Using a small metal device, the spring clip end held the paper, allowing him to shake out tobacco evenly from the pouch. Next, the instrument rolled the cigarette, and he licked the paper to seal the edge. Then, he passed the smoke through a round hole at the other end of the device, assuring a calibrated uniformity. Finally, he tamped the smoke against the metal surface, tightly packing the tobacco. Only then did he light it, blowing a blue cloud of smoke toward the ceiling.

Along with his workers in the mine, he hired men as enforcers, and Captain Vogel was the leader. Thorne knew the man's size and his shrewdness in handling men were legendary throughout the mining camps and, probably, clear up to Grants Pass. *It helps him in tackling enforcement jobs,* Cort thought, *just like he did last night in the mine tunnel.*

As Vogel made his way to the back of the saloon, Thorne continued thinking about his growing cache of gold. *And then all my treasure has to be safely transported one hundred-sixty miles to the landing on the Sacramento River at Red Buff. From there, it goes by steamship to the mint in San Francisco. Yes, my men have many things to watch. Wonder if the captain is getting too old for this line of work. I'd better keep an eye on him, as the bandits around here are becoming more daring.*

"Evening, Captain," the mine owner said. "Pull up a chair and sit yourself."

"How do," Renke replied, laying his black hat on the table. Pulling around a chair, he sat down.

"Pour yourself a drink."

"Don't mind if I do."

"Besides all the whooping and hollering at the tables, there's been no trouble tonight from these sourdoughs."

Renke nodded, savoring the shot of quality whiskey, which the mine owner ordinarily reserved for his own use.

"You were productive last night. The one you tied up at the mine entrance was hanged this morning."

The captain remained silent, his eyes flitting over the crowd.

Lowering his voice, Thorne leaned forward and continued, "There'll be a pack train of burros ready to travel on

Thursday morning for Red Bluff. It's the biggest shipment yet, and I want you to head the guard detail."

"Sorry, I've got personal business over the Siskiyou Mountains, in Grants Pass, and I'm booked on the morning stage."

"What the hell are you talking about?" Cort hissed, voicing his knife-edged anger. "It's a ten-day trip to the landing on the river, and you know better than anyone, that there are a thousand places along the trail for an ambush. What in damnation is this business in Grants Pass? Is there something I should know?"

"Nope."

"Well, postpone it. You can't leave me high and dry. There'll be over fifty thousand dollars in high-grade ore and gold dust in the train, and I want my best men guarding it. You've heard the same reports that I have, about outlaws waylaying shipments in these mountains from other mining camps. I ain't taking any chances."

His chief enforcer stared at him for a moment, then said, "Last week, I told you I had personal business in Grants Pass, and you didn't mention anything about this shipment. You have enough men to guard it without me. Pick someone else to lead it."

In a harsh, raspy whisper, Thorne replied, "This is the biggest delivery I've ever sent, and, by God, you're going to lead it."

"I understand your concern," Renke replied, running his fingers through his collar-length hair. The big man rocked back in his chair and scratched his white beard.

"What in damnation is this personal business in Grants Pass, anyway, and why the hell do you have to leave tomorrow?"

"It's private, and I've made plans."

"This train is too important to me. You *will* lead it."

"I told you . . ."

Butting in, Cort asked, "How long have you been working for me, Vogel?"

"Going on three years."

"I gave you a job when some said you were too old and over the hill," Thorne raged. "You'll damn well lead this shipment! Otherwise, you can clear out from these diggings for good. And that means right now!"

Slowly, Renke brought his chair down to the floor, never taking his eyes off him. Softly, he said, "Now, let's keep our tempers, Mr. Cort. No need you getting all frothy on the matter."

He sensed a hint of menace and knew that the man sitting across from him had a hair-trigger disposition, sometimes giving way to violent mood swings. The captain explained them away as "letting out my passions." It was best to stay off his path during such occurrences. Cort suddenly felt a chill go down his back. *Despite Vogel's age and white hair, he could kill me in an instant, walk out of my saloon, and I'll wager that not one damn sourdough would be man enough to stand in his way.* In seeming innocence, he moved the cane on the table, pointing the end toward his big enforcer.

Just as casually, the captain poured himself another drink and set the bottle down between him and the tip of the walking stick.

Reacting unconsciously, the saloon owner pushed his chair farther from the edge of the table, screeching the legs against the plank floor. Forcing himself to appear at ease, he said, "Look, Renke, I figure you're due for a bonus. Take care of this job and you can take some time off."

Coolly, the captain replied, "Have it your way, this time, Mr. Cort." The big man rose and strode out of the smoky saloon and into the night, as the relentlessly harsh sound of the stamping mill filled the air.

CHAPTER EIGHTEEN

Captain Vogel's big gray horse climbed to the top of a ridge, and he scanned the trail ahead with his field glass. In a narrow gulch below, burros were on lead ropes strung in two lines, with a heavy pack on each animal. From the hill, he watched as one of his men headed each string of animals, while other guards were outriders on all sides of the gold train.

Renke shifted uncomfortably on his horse. In recent months, the pains in his backside and groin were more troubling. A few weeks earlier, the saddler in town finished building a new saddle for him that lengthened the seat by shifting the cantle and angling the pommel forward. It allowed him to vary his position on long rides, which eased the pains. Consoling himself, he thought, *Well, I'll just have to see Doctor John Samuels in Grants Pass after this delivery. He'll fix me up with more laudanum for my aches, as he's done before. Meanwhile, this new saddle and lamb's wool padding make for an easier ride.*

The journey south would take a week, as the train traveled over the Siskiyou Trail, which curled between high mountain peaks. First blazed by fur traders for the *Hudson's Bay Company*, the route passed on the west side of Mount Shasta, along Strawberry Valley and down to Poverty Flats on the flatlands. If the weather held, another three days would see them arriving at Red Bluff, the most northern, navigable port on the Sacramento River. From there, the gold traveled on the steamboat *Orient,* to be refined and turned into coins, or stored as bullion, at the San Francisco Mint.

Renke realized that there was no way of keeping this train's departure a secret in Yreka, as rumors and news sped rapidly through every mining camp. His assumption was that any outlaw interested in the shipment knew the timing and likely had someone watching all the preparations.

His deduction did not make him overly nervous about this particular trip, as he had eighteen guards, all armed with rifles or shotguns, and some also carried pistols. It would take a large band of men to carry out a robbery against such a force. Yet, it was always possible.

As he shifted in the saddle again to ease himself, he rode over a hilltop and down the backside, a route that took him to the bottom of a small draw, which eventually intersected with the main trail.

In the distance, the permanently snow-covered peaks of Mount Shasta rose majestically, which were visible to travelers for days, from any direction. In the ancient Karuk language of a long-ago Indian tribe, Shasta meant "white mountain." *A most fitting name,* he mused. *Cloud shadows passing across the mountain's white slopes are surely an amazing and changing picture book of God's mighty design. And today, I also see "Little Shasta," and its black, rocky cone guarding the western flank of the big peaks.*

Waiting for the train to appear around a bend, the shockwave of a large explosion struck him. Almost immediately, he heard gunshots, and his horse anxiously reared. Reining the animal about, he spurred the gray and galloped toward his men.

As he rounded a bend, he heard the whine of ricocheting bullets. Ahead, the blast had tumbled the hillside in front of the burros. Riding through the smoke and dust over the new ridge, he saw that several of his riders were already lying on the ground. Others were attempting to turn the pack animals around, while shooting at men hidden behind rocks and trees on both sides.

Suddenly, there was a second detonation behind the train. Front and rear, they were corralled between the steep sides of the canyon and the newly formed barriers.

Spinning his horse about, he galloped away from the scene and found a way up the difficult slope to get above the outlaws. In short order, he neared the crest and stopped. Pulling his rifle, he dismounted and ran among the rocks until he had a clear view of the action below. Dismayed, he saw that many of his men were down.

Some attempted to ride over the blockade at the rear, only to be shot by riflemen hidden on the higher ridges. Others took cover and returned the bandits' fire. The whole train was in peril.

Easing down the hill, he surprised a bandit who was crouched behind a tree. With a swift uppercut with the butt of his rifle, he flattened the man.

To his right, he heard more shooting. Making his way in that direction, he came upon three outlaws, each firing down at his men.

Immediately, they saw him and scrambled to their feet.

Renke's knife flew through the air, burying itself in one man's chest, and his pistol shot felled another.

The third bandit swung his rifle like a club, hitting the captain across the back of the neck with the gunstock.

Renke staggered, trying to recover, and fumbled, cocking his Colt six-shooter again.

A second blow to the head laid him out.

* * *

As Renke Vogel slowly opened his eyes and tried to focus, the sun was setting behind the stark distant peaks called Castle Crags, which jutted oddly into the sky. He struggled to a kneeling position, his head hurting like blazing fury. He gingerly touched a hand to the back of his neck and felt dried blood. Using his rifle for assistance, he slowly stood.

A man was lying nearby with a knife buried in his chest and another with a gunshot wound to the head. After retrieving his big blade, he searched their pockets, but found nothing that identified them or the gang.

Shaking his head increased the pain, and he steadied himself against a tree until the dizziness passed. Renke struggled to walk uphill toward his horse. Looking down into the canyon, he saw no sign of the pack animals or the bandits, while riderless horses grazed near a steam running along the bottom. His men lay scattered on the ground. Gradually, a dark rage of fury began to build within him.

Reaching the clearing, the man he had clubbed was still unconscious, with a nasty gash on the side of his head. Pulling off the outlaw's belt, he bound his hands and searched him, again finding nothing of note. He retrieved his horse, as the bandit regained consciousness. Roughly, Renke lifted him to his feet.

The outlaw let out a low moan of pain.

"You'll live. What's your name?"

The man glowered.

"I'm only going to ask you one more time. What's your name?"

"Slade."

"Well, Mr. Slade, we're going to make our way down this hill," Renke said, mounting his horse and throwing a rope over the outlaw. Prodding the man with his rifle, they made it to the bottom, where he tied the captive to a tree.

Quickly, he rode up and down the trail in the *arroyo*, but there was no sign of life, until he heard a sound and hurried to a fallen man hidden behind large rocks. Turning him over, Renke found a sorry mess. *Sam won't make it through the night,* he figured. Carrying the wounded man to a spot near the outlaw, he collected wood and started a fire.

Untying Slade and waving his pistol menacingly, he commanded, "Start collecting the bodies of my men, then roundup more wood for the campfire. And, by the way, try anything, and I'll shoot your knee off, but that'll be just an instant before I shoot you through the heart."

Resentfully, Slade went about the task. Then, they both herded the horses together and picketed them to a line strung between two trees.

"All right, Slade, back to your tree.

With a surly look, the man sat with his back against the tree.

After securing the outlaw again, Renke counted the horses. *Damnation, every pony here accounts for my men plus the bandits who were killed. That means that there'll be none returning to give the alarm in Yreka, and no posse will be raised, at least not for a long while. If I ride back to town now, I'll lose two days, and this gang will slip farther away, perhaps for good.*

Returning to the fire, he made a pallet of blankets for the wounded man. Covering him and wiping down his face with a damp neckerchief, he asked, "Sam, did you get a look at any of the outlaws? Did you recognize anyone?"

The injured man struggled to talk but lost consciousness.

Renke squatted beside the creek and washed the dried blood off his head and neck. His head hurt like hell, and he was unsteady when he stood, as pain shot through his backside and thigh.

He approached the trussed-up bandit and saw the man looking at him, a sneer on his face. "Where're they taking the gold, Slade?"

"Go to hell. You'll never get anything out of me."

Staring at him for a moment, he pulled his long hunting knife from its sheath.

The man's eyes grew bigger, but he managed to retain his scornful look.

"You want a little sobering truth? The plains Indians have a habit of burying a man in a hole with only his head showing. Then, they douse him with honey and let the ants and scorpions feast. It not only makes a man talk, but it assures his long-drawn-out, agonizing death."

"You're a big talker, old man," the bandit replied. "When my *compadres* come back for me, it'll be you that I'll enjoy killing, real slow-like."

"Well, I'm a bit more civilized than them Indians," Renke continued, ignoring the comment, "and I'm not in favor of long rituals that take days. As for your partners, they got the burros with the gold, and they'll figure that a big posse will be after them soon. They've already forgotten about you, Slade, and you're a damn fool if you think otherwise."

His words had no effect, as the man continued to stare at him defiantly. "Have it your way," Renke said. "Later, we'll get back to our little talk."

"You're wasting your time, old man."

Muddle-headed, he walked to the creek and splashed water on his face, then returned to the fire with his saddlebags. Taking out a piece of deer jerky, he sat and chewed, hoping that the spinning and throbbing in his head would stop. After seeing to the wounded man again, he lay on his bedroll. He was dead tired and was soon asleep.

With a start, Renke awoke. The campfire was reduced to glowing embers, and every sense alerted him that something was stirring about. Quietly rolling out of his covering, he drew his pistol and looked toward the bandit. In the light of a full moon, Slade was still sitting on the ground, his back to the tree, with his head slumped on his chest. But, on the other side of camp, Sam was gone. *Where in holy tarnation did he go?*

Standing slowly, he carefully looked around the camp, then heard noises coming from the creek. Walking toward the sounds, he saw the wounded man lying with his head partially in the water.

"Sam, what're you doing? It's me, Renke Vogel."

"Captain, I was thirsty and heard the running water."

"Did you get a look at any of them bandits?"

"Not a one," Sam managed to say. "We came down the gulch and didn't see anything until the first explosion. They planned the ambush well and opened fire on us from both hillsides." He said, gritting his teeth. "How bad is my wound?"

"It ain't good. C'mon, I'll help you back to your blanket."

Before sunrise, Sam died. Renke rolled him in a bedroll and lashed the ends with leather strips.

At first light, he felt more refreshed, although his head still hurt and a huge welt ran across his ear and neck. A pot of coffee was steaming near the fire, and he sat chewing jerky, thinking about his next move. *I have to let Cort know what's happened to the gold shipment, so he can raise a posse.* As he thought through a plan, his rage returned over the loss of his men.

Slade was awake on the other side of the campfire, staring at him with all the hostility he could muster.

Rising, Captain Renke said, "Let's continue our talk from yesterday. Where're they taking the gold?"

"I told you once and I'll say it again, go to hell."

"All right, I can tell that you're going to be hard-headed, so we best see if I can make you more obliging."

"My friends are returning soon," Slade snarled, "and when we're through with you, you'll be asking us to put you out of your misery."

"Could be, but I'm thinking they're long gone with the gold, and have forgotten about you and your share of the loot," Renke said, freeing his large hunting knife from its sheaf. With a startlingly quick underhand throw, it flashed through the air and buried itself, with a loud thud, above the bandit's head.

Startled, the man's eyes rose to stare at the quivering, silver blade stuck in the tree trunk.

"Let's start again. Where're they taking the gold?"

"You big ox, you don't scare me, old man," Slade replied, with a tremor in his voice.

"I'm a God-fearing man, and you're forcing me to do things against my beliefs. So, you have no one to blame but yourself." He walked over and retrieved the knife, with quick up and down jerks. He then moved toward the fire. Quickly, he turned and his next throw sliced the outside of the man's thigh.

"*Ahh*," the man yelled, "you calf-brain, mother's son of . . ."

"Control yourself, you murdering thief." Again, he freed his knife.

The howling man thrashed about in pain, blood streaming from the wound.

"You know, a couple more cuts like that, and you're going to bleed to death before the sun rises over that ridge. So, lets you and I talk about the gold?"

"You lamebrain, boot-licking bastard, I'm a lot tougher than you think. I expect my partners will be here any time now." With increasing bravado, he continued, "Then, maybe I'll use your suggestion and bury you up to your neck and let the critters do their work."

"You're a damn stubborn cuss, aren't you? Well, it's no skin off my backside. I hope I miss and don't hit your private parts this time." Deliberately exaggerating and pretending to throw, he saw the man squirm and throw his legs to one side.

"Seeing as you're moving about, how about I try to pin your ear to the tree behind you. Will that ease some of your worries?"

The bandit was beside himself, and, despite the chill in the morning air, he was sweating. "Do your worst," he yelled. "I'm not talking."

"Just as you like, Mr. Slade." The next throw grazed the man's head, nicking the scalp. As Renke watched, blood from the wound flowed down the bandit's neck. Recovering his knife, the big man continued, "This could be fun, even though it's against my beliefs. I throw pretty well for an old cougar, don't I? You want to pick another target for me?"

"You'll get no information from me," the outlaw screamed, his voice full of venom.

Quicker than the eye, the captain wheeled and the next throw landed next to the man's crotch.

That broke the outlaw's bravado. "All right, you chicken-livered bastard, I'll talk if you promise to let me go."

"I make the terms," Renke replied, his voice laced with anger. "You tell me now, or my next throw is going to pin your other ear to the tree." Raising his booming voice, he commanded, "Where're they taking the gold?"

"You have to promise that you won't cut me any more."

He leaned over the man, holding his knife close to the bandit's eyes. "Go on, tell me what I want to know, and do it now."

"We were holed up in a cave at the foot of a place called Castle Crags."

"Isn't that near the beginnings of the Sacramento River?"

"That's right."

"And that's where the gang is headed with the gold?"

"I ain't sure," the outlaw hedged.

With a loud growl like an angry grizzly, Captain Vogel shouted, "What the hell do you mean, you ain't sure? Are they going back there or not? Speak up, man, because my patience with you has done run out."

"I heard talk that stealing such a big shipment was bound to draw a large posse, and it'd be best to stay off the traveled routes. It was decided that we'd lose our tracks in the large lava fields northeast of Mount Shasta and then head south, down the other side of the mountain. We figured that no one would think to look for us in that wild country."

"How many men are there in the gang?"

The outlaw grimaced with pain. "There were twenty-one, when we started."

I got three including this fellow, he figured, *and my men killed six others. So, I'm chasing a dozen outlaws.*

"Much obliged for your assistance," Renke said, as he wrapped neckerchiefs around the outlaw's wounds. He had already determined that there was only one possible way in getting word of the ambush to Yreka.

Untying the man, he commanded, "Throw each of my men over a pony's saddle, and see that they're tied on good and proper."

"Mister, I'm hurting too bad," Slade complained.

Instantly, Renke knocked him to the ground with a right fist. Standing over him, he unclenched and clenched his large hands. The loss of his men gnawed at him, and he was at the edge with this gunslinger. "One more word and

I'll gut you right here in this *arroyo*. Now, tell me quick, are you going to follow my orders?"

The outlaw got to his feet and made his way to the first dead man, dragging along his injured leg and muttering obscenities under his breath.

"And make it fast!"

When the task was completed, the captain went down the line of horses, tying the reins of each animal to the tail of another and checking the ropes securing his men. He manhandled Slade atop the last horse and quickly hog-tied his legs with a rope under the horse's belly. Then, he whipped it around his hands and tied them to the saddle horn.

"No, you can't leave me tied like this," the outlaw, screamed. "You promised to let me go."

"Uh-huh, slim chance of that," Renke grunted, busily writing a note. Using a knife from one of the fallen men, he tacked the note to the saddle of the lead horse. He hoped that someone would come across the large string of animals and raise the alarm.

The outlaw was fuming. "You made a promise to me. Hell, if these horses make it back to town, those folks will hang me, you stinking son of a whore."

"That's about right," he acknowledged. "Have an enjoyable ride, Mr. Slade. Aha, get moving," he yelled, slapping the front horse across the rump with the flat of his rifle. "Yip, yip, get along! *Adios, amigo,*" he saluted, smacking the outlaw's horse with the rifle butt, as the line of animals went over the ridge created by the first explosion.

With his stallion saddled, Captain Renke Vogel turned to follow the outlaws' trail.

CHAPTER NINETEEN

Renke rode hard, though the stabs of pain in his butt increased, yet there was no letup, as the gray horse covered mile after mile throughout the day. While the gang had a considerable head start, the slow pace of the burros hindered their progress. From a ridge, he saw a dust cloud far to the east in the last light of the day. *That's got to be the gang*, he surmised.

The slopes of Mount Shasta glowed in the setting sun, reflecting shades of reds and dazzling yellows. Then, night began overtaking the high summits, as vibrant colors turned to purple tinges, and dark shadows slowly veiled canyons and valleys.

I have damn few alternatives from here on out, he figured. *If I simply follow and catch up, I could ride right into the gang and be ambushed again. They'll eventually turn south and head down the east side of the big mountain, as Slade said, where they'll encounter few travelers. Perhaps, I could get ahead of them by cutting the dogleg and riding* southeast. *By Jove, I have a full moon tonight, and it may be possible. That would allow me to plan my own welcoming party for these murdering gents.*

Dismounting, he attempted to walk off his stiffness while making camp and unsaddling his horse. From his tote bag, he pulled out the last bottle of laudanum. After a long pull, he carefully repacked the half-full bottle. *I'll stay here for a few hours until the moon is high. It'll do me good to eat some jerky and rest for a bit. I know my horse needs it, too.*

He figured it was after midnight when he mounted the gray again and began the next leg of his quest. In the clear night sky, he picked out the two stars in the Big Dipper's cup that point to the North Star, then took a fix on other stars, to guide him southeast.

He had no illusions. Even if he intercepted the murdering outlaws, he was one man against a dozen. Not even trickery would be enough against so many guns. Yet, the thought of turning back was not his way.

For the next five hours, he kept a steady pace. Many times, he dismounted and led his horse, as the ground became too uneven and the bright moonlight was insufficient to ride safely. Taking new bearings from the sky, he rode on, through the early-morning darkness, as moonlight reflected off the white slopes of Mount Shasta, and hues of silver-gray peeked from the rest of the impenetrable blackness. His increasing stiffness was an issue, but there was nothing more to be done, as he figured it better to save his remaining laudanum.

False dawn came over the land as he crested a hill and reined in, astonished at the sight of a large herd of cattle spread out below him, with distant cowpokes riding along the far edge. To his left, he saw the glow of a morning campfire.

He was confused. *This can't be the outlaw bunch, can it? Punching cows doesn't exactly fit with men on the run, trying to make time, and thinking a big posse is tracking them. So, who are these folks? And where in bloody hell did they come from, camped here in the middle of nowhere, with no one around for a hundred or more miles in any direction of the compass? Maybe I'm just too tired and seeing things that make no sense,* he reasoned.

He took out his glass and studied the camp for an eternity through the high-powered lens. All seemed to be peaceful, just as one would expect of cowboys driving cattle. He saw men gathered about the fire, and they seemed to be following a normal, early-morning routine. Groggy and tired, he judged, *they must be headed to the mining camps and, most likely, Yreka, as it's the largest.* He looked through his glass again, trying to count the number of men. *There must be a dozen or more drovers in that group.*

Suddenly, a new thought occurred to him. *If Yreka is their destination, this cattle drive will be heading northwest, right towards the outlaws coming their way. Damnation, these folks have a decent chance of being massacred, just like my men.*

The thought spurred him to action, as his heels prodded his tired horse into a gallop. Approaching the encampment, he slowed and shouted, "Hello, the camp. I'm a lone rider. Can I approach the campfire?"

"State your business, stranger," a voice answered.

"My name is Captain Renke Vogel, and I'm part of a posse from Yreka."

There was a long pause and then the voice called out, "Approach, mister, but make no sudden moves."

Nearing, he was surprised to see two large wagons, fully loaded and covered with canvas tarps. Even more unexpected was the sight of a woman approaching him, holding a rifle pointed at him.

"Me name is Lisa Annie Sparks. What's your business hereabouts?"

"As I said, I'm a lawman. I work for Thorne Cort, the owner of the Sourdough Wind Mine in Yreka. Two days ago, a gang of outlaws waylaid my pack train of animals and gunned down eighteen of my men. I got a late start chasing after them, but they're slowed down by the burros carrying heavy ore packs. I rode half the night across country to cut ahead of them."

A well-built cowpuncher pushed through the group and stood staring at him.

Renke returned his stare. *Funny, there's something familiar about this young fellow.*

"Get down stranger and share breakfast with us," the drover said.

Glad to be out of the saddle, he replied wearily, "That's a generous offer, and I accept. My backside is more than a little stiff after my hard ride the last few days, and the coffee and frying bacon smell mighty fine."

Approaching, the same man offered his hand.

As they shook, Renke was startled when the younger man continued to hold his hand in a strong grip.

Still staring at him, the man said, "Please tell me your name once more."

"It's Captain Renke Vogel."

Never letting go of Renke's hand, the cowpuncher studied him, then asked, "Could it be that you're from Missouri? You wouldn't be from the lands back there called Six Bulls, would you?"

Renke was taken aback. "Why do you ask such a question?" he responded, now scrutinizing the other man with keen interest. "And how is it that you know Six Bulls country?"

Breaking into a big smile and still holding his hand, the man replied, "Because I know a man by your name that I haven't seen in many years. Uncle Renke, don't you recognize me? I'm your nephew, Jonah Sommer."

The morning had begun with one surprise after another, as recognition slowly came to him. Smiling, he answered, "Forgive me, son, as I surely didn't recognize you, now that you're all grown up. My, you've become a tall and broad-shouldered fellow. And to boot, you're the last man I'd expect to run across in this wild country."

Jonah grabbed the big man in a bear hug. "I swear, I've never been so glad to see anyone more in my whole life. Back home, Pa was always talking about you. Do you recall my younger brother, Frank, or maybe you'd remember him by the name we called him in Missouri, Francis Marion? He was too young to remember you before you left Six Bulls." Turning around, he saw his brother. "Frank, come shake hands with your Uncle Renke, known to all as Captain Renke Vogel."

The teenager shook the captain's hand, apparently struck dumb to be in the presence of a legend that he had heard about all his life.

"I'm glad to see you again, young man," Renke said, trying to hide his embarrassment at not recognizing the boys. "Can we sit by the fire and talk? I'm sure anxious for that cup of coffee, and your frying bacon smells heavenly. My fingers are half froze from riding most of the night."

Jonah introduced Mrs. Sparks, Lem, and some of the others nearby. The next few minutes were spent in a happy reunion.

"Captain, where in tarnation are you headed?" Jonah finally asked. "And tell me again what brings you to this wild country?"

Lisa Annie and the others gathered around, listening.

"I was leading a train of burros carrying gold ore a few days back. It was headed south on the other side of the big mountain, down to the port of Red Bluff on the Sacramento River. From there, the shipment was to journey downriver by steamer to the mint in San Francisco. A day out of Yreka, bandits ambushed us. In the battle, all my men were killed, and I was knocked on the head, so I didn't get on their trail until yesterday morning. I assume you're headed toward the camps northwest of Mount Shasta with this herd, like the gold-mining camp of Yreka. Am I right?"

"Yep."

"For every last one of you, a terrible danger is coming your way."

"What kind of danger?"

"I believe that these murdering outlaws will kill anyone crossing their path to keep their trail hidden."

"Where are they bound?"

"I don't rightly know their final destination. Probably, it's somewhere around the Sacramento Delta, or maybe elsewhere. I captured one bandit, who told me that the gang planned to head northeast to lose their trail in the lava fields. Then, they planned to go down this side of the big mountain to avoid being seen by travelers. The short of it is, you're going north, and they're headed south. You'll likely cross paths about mid-day.

Jonah listened quietly to the explanation.

"This is a big shipment of gold ore," Renke continued, "and the gang has to assume that a large posse will be chasing after them."

"Is there a posse on their trail?"

"If there isn't, there will be. With all my men dead, I sent their horses off with the one thief I captured tied to the saddle. I'm figuring that someone will come across them and carry the news back to Yreka. If not, it will take even more time for any chase to begin."

"So, you're a posse of one. How many outlaws are there?"

"About a dozen men, according to the one I talked with."

"Just how much gold did they get away with, Captain Vogel?" Lisa Annie asked.

"It's worth fifty thousand dollars, *más o menos.*"

"Oh, sweet Jesus, keep us from temptation and save us from the devil," she said, making a sign of the cross.

Renke saw the look of wonder on their faces. "And," he continued, making an instant decision, "the reward for the safe return of the shipment is five thousand dollars."

"Yahoo," Frank shouted, "let's go get them."

Renke continued, "Jonah, if you and your party are willing to help me, I'll swear all of you in as deputies. But hear me good, this isn't any lark excursion for the faint-hearted. These men are dangerous cutthroats."

Jonah stared at him before speaking, "It seems that we have little choice. With the herd, we can't easily hide or change direction, and our trail dust can be seen from a long way off. I guess we'll have to see how fate deals the cards. Now, come have some breakfast. We have the usual, beans and biscuits. We can also rustle up more bacon to satisfy your appetite, and I was just about to crush more beans to make another pot of coffee."

"Much obliged, Jonah."

CHAPTER TWENTY

Freshly mounted, Captain Vogel and Jonah journeyed northwest for more than an hour and stopped on a hill. From this vantage point, he viewed the area to the north with his glass, looking for anything that indicated a large group heading south. He swept the field once, then again, and stopped.

"I see a faint dust trail in the sky, Jonah," Renke said, handing the lens to his nephew. "Here, see for yourself. Look about three points to the left of that distant mountain peak. That bit of dust in the air must be the outlaws."

"You may be right, sir. Now what?"

"Let's sit a spell until we can make sure that it's heading our way."

Over the next half-hour, the two sat under the shade of a rock, with their unsaddled horses nosing about in the low-growing grass.

After a while, Jonah asked, "How do you happen to be in this part of California?"

"After I left Missouri, I just tried to put the bad times behind me. I kicked around some in Denver, but the stories about gold in California brought me farther west."

The two sat in silence, warmed by the sun.

"Tell me about Missouri." Renke finally said. "I'd like to understand why you and Frank took a mind to leave. Was this a quick decision that you boys made? Did you have a chance to say good-bye to your pa?"

"Ah, sort of—you see, it was sudden-like."

Renke listened as his nephew told him about their departure. He tried to picture Frank's reactions at the family picnic, when his father announced his intent to marry the boy's sweetheart. And later, Frank confronted the girl and learned about the farmhand's attack and her expected child.

Jonah continued, describing his brother's anguish and bitterness at the news, resulting in their leaving the same night, with only a brief note to their father. He ended by telling Renke the amazing last episode of the story, and how Curtis, their oldest brother, hunted down the attacker. He searched for weeks with no luck, until the evil farmhand went on a killing spree. On the banks of the Platte River, his brother finally overtook the man during a fight to the finish.

In the warmth of the sun, the two men continued to sit quietly on the hilltop.

Renke finally broke the silence. "The world ain't a perfect place. Fortunately, most people get on with their lives, and let others do the same. If danger is about, folks take steps to survive and protect themselves and their families. On occasion, you encounter someone who is ruthless and so lacking in any human qualities that it makes your hair stand on end. Looking for trouble isn't the way to live. Even so, if it does come, there's no use tucking it in and running.

In simple terms, you deal with it. Sounds like Curtis did just that"

"Uh-huh, those are my views, too. You ever run into folks like that?"

"More than once," he replied, thinking about Thorne Cort. He added, "You'll recall that I did have a reason for leaving Six Bulls country?"

"Ah, yes, sir. I didn't mean to bring up a sore point."

"Pay no mind. Let's take another look through the glass."

They determined that the cloud was indeed headed their way.

"My young nephew, I believe that is the dust trail of the gang. Let's head back to the herd. I'd like to look for a place to meet these murderers and give them a little surprise, like they did to my men and me."

Riding hard, they traveled until they gauged they were halfway between the herd and the outlaws.

"See those two low-lying hills?" Renke asked. "Let's ride to the top of the one on the left."

Dismounting on the knoll, both men surveyed the confined valley below. The ground showed signs of prior use, with wagon ruts deeply etched in the hardpan. It was a natural passage for anyone heading south or north.

Renke asked, "How good are you and your men with rifles?"

"I'm not sure about the drovers, but I'm a fair shot, and Frank is a deadeye. Gene and Alex are former cavalry troopers, so I'd say that we have at least four experienced shooters."

"I think I have a plan," he said. "Let's ride back to the others."

Before mid-day, Jonah's men and the herd neared the twin hills. Stopping outside the southern entrance to the small valley, everyone gathered together.

Jonah glanced at his uncle. No one had put his uncle in charge, yet the mantle of leadership fell easily on him. "Tell us what you have in mind, sir."

Looking over the group, Renke said, "Well, you see, the idea is not to get any of us killed. Surprise is on our side, and we're going to take full advantage of it. Jonah and Gene," the big man ordered, "you take positions on the hill to the west. Frank, you and Alex get atop the other one. Lem, you and the rest of the men hold the cows here. I'll ride north to the other end of the valley and hide until the gold train has passed my position. Then, I'll open fire from the rear. Lem, that'll be the signal to stampede the herd, cutting off this end of their route. You boys on the hills open fire and shoot at any of the murderers who come into range. I figure we'll have them in one hell of a boxed-in ambush. Anybody got anything else to add?"

"What about me and the wagons?" Lisa Annie asked.

"Ma'am, I'd prefer that you stay with the wagons, out of danger."

"Isn't every one of us in harm's way, me dear captain?" she asked, in her lilting voice.

Renke was taken aback. "No offense meant, Mrs. Sparks. Do you have another suggestion?"

"Me and the wagons should quickly follow the herd into the pass. That'll raise even more dust in the sky and likely make our group look larger. Don't ye agree, me good man?"

Captain Vogel looked at the woman for a moment and then nodded. "I guess we can give it a try. Are there any more ideas? All right, I'm off for my place. God be with us." Reining his gray about, he galloped off, slapping his horse's haunches with his black hat.

Jonah and Gene followed, taking cover behind a maze of boulders near the hill's highest ridge. Jonah saw his brother and Alex doing the same across the way. The captain was out of sight, far to his right, and the herd of cattle milled at the other end of the valley. In the distance, the rising dust trail marked the progress of the gold train.

Jonah rested, sitting with his back against a large rock, and watched the snail-paced progress of the outlaws. In the heat of the midday sun, he let his thoughts return to the last time he saw his uncle in Missouri.

It must have been at least a dozen years ago, he reflected. More and more folks were coming to southwest Missouri, in search of virgin farmland that they could purchase from the U.S. Government for five bits an acre.

Our town had been recently platted, attracting merchants and stores to the growing farming valley, and to the business done with passing wagon trains. These caravans mostly originated in southern states, and traffic through the farming area was not heavy. Yet, every spring, it was steady and growing, as more folks migrated to the western frontier. This breathed greater demand for food and leather items produced in Six Bulls country.

On a bright, sunny Saturday afternoon so long ago, folks gathered from around the county to celebrate the founding of the new town. In an unusual quirk, the community was undecided on a name for the new village. Untroubled, the celebration went ahead, with free beer and spit-roasted beef, as well as contests for the best pie, sack and wheelbarrow races for youngsters. And, at the end of the afternoon, a horse race was held that took the riders around the new town twice. His half-Indian cousin, Seneca, won, crossing the finish line with his dark hair and braid flying behind him in the wind.

The hoot-and-belch crowd, a term Pa used for the drunken rabble that day, began acting up. Loudly carrying on, and under the influence of the free-flowing beer, they started hurling insults at Seneca and his new bride, Flower on the Water, because they were Indians.

The two young people ignored the bullies and prepared to leave.

Suddenly, one riffraff uncoiled his bullwhip and began cursing and lashing Seneca. Recovering, his cousin got the better of the man, only to be shot dead by another ruffian.

The turn of events stunned everyone and a deathly hush fell over the crowd, broken by the lone, mournful wailing of Flower on the Water, as she cradled her dead husband in her arms.

That's when Uncle Renke charged into the gathering on his stallion and confronted the dozen or so beer-guzzling men. Dismounting, his hunting knife hissed through the air, finding its mark in the shooter's throat. In my head, I can still picture the knife's long blade flashing in the sunlight, as it flew to its target. Before hitting the ground, the man was dead, his face frozen in a startled expression, with his eyes wide open.

Then, the captain challenged the man with the whip in a hand-to-hand battle, causing the crowd to move back. Punches were traded, but clearly, Uncle Renke was the stronger of the two and a more skilled fighter. It ended when he picked the rowdy up, raised him above his head, and brought him down hard and fast against his knee, which he thrust upward. Slowly, the man slipped to the ground, jerking uncontrollably in the spasms of death.

Jonah winched, recalling the distinct sound of the man's spine snapping.

Next, my uncle turned to face the rest of the beer-guzzling group. Swaying slightly on the balls of his feet, he angrily said, "I'm this young man's friend, and I'm an Indian-lover. So what're you going to do about it?"

The rowdies remained motionless, shocked by the quick and unexpected deaths of their friends.

Uncle Renke continued his taunting. "Could be that you're just big-talking, silly milkmaids, long ago castrated, and pretending to be a rough and tumble fellow like me." Not satisfied with their lack of response, he demanded, "Come on, are there any real men among you? Or maybe you're all cowards with pig droppings for brains."

The large gathering of people stood stunned and in absolute silence. No one moved. There was no cough, no spoken word, not even the rustle of clothes. Everyone stood transfixed by the fast-paced events and the brutality of the three deaths.

Unsatisfied, Uncle Renke roared again, "What's it to be, gents? I'll take you one at a time or all at once." Then, in a low voice edged with the chill of death, he had continued, "And I mean to kill every last one of you bastards."

Jonah recalled the faces of the troublemakers. *They quickly sobered as they confronted the shroud of their own death. All stood stock-still, faces pale, and some with mouths agape. On the pain of likely death, none made eye contact with my uncle.*

"The only way to save yourselves on this here day, is to leave town right now and never, ever come back."

The rowdies remained motionless, still in shock, as the air hung thick with tension.

Once more, the big captain roared, "What's it to be? You leaving or dying?"

One bent down, intending to collect the dead shooter.

"Let him be, damn you to hell," the captain shouted, in his bear-like voice. "Are you leaving this instant, or do I have to kill the lot of you, beginning with you?" he said, taking a step forward and pointing at the one who wanted to collect his friend.

The group quickly turned and ran for their horses. Mounting, the rowdies left, galloping out of town, as the crowd watched them depart.

Almost as one, the gathering turned back once more to my uncle, who stood looking down at the two dead ruffians. Shaking his head, he said, in his husky voice, "Better bury this trash deep. We don't want to disease the local coyotes."

Mounting his horse, the big man addressed the crowd of farmers and merchants. "We've had too much hatred and killing between Indians and white folks. The new town needs a proper name, and I think it should be forever called 'Seneca' to honor the memory of my young, half-breed friend." He waited, looking around. "Is there anyone who objects?"

No one spoke or gave any sign.

Touching the brim of his hat as a parting salute, he walked his horse out of the new village of Seneca, heading west. He looked neither right nor left, just straight ahead, as the crowd parted before him. No one tried to stop him. None stood in his path. Most men even avoided looking him in the eye.

Until this morning, it was the last time I saw him, but his deeds in the land of the Six Bulls became a legend throughout southwest Missouri.

Rousing himself, Jonah looked north, up the trail. The dust cloud marking the gang's approach was close, and he tightly clutched his rifle. The midday sun was hot in the cloudless sky, as drops of sweat ran down his back. He removed his hat to be less conspicuous and untied his bandana, using it to wipe his brow and clammy hands.

He watched as the outlaw band finally entered the valley. The leader's clothes were covered with trail dust, and he wore a wide-brimmed hat and leather coat. Smoking a *cigarrillo*, the man's black beard glistened in the bright sunlight.

As the man rode by, Jonah waited expectantly for the signal, flexing his fingers to relieve the strain. In the next instant, he heard a gunshot, and he fired at a rider, knocking the man out of his saddle.

Immediately, others opened fire and he heard the roar of distant guns, as Lem and the drovers began stampeding the cattle into the narrow opening. He reloaded quickly and fired, missing his next target. Four or five outlaws were already down, as he reloaded once more.

From his right, he caught sight of the captain hurtling out of the brush, his hat flying off his head and his white hair glistening in the glaring sun. There was a rifle in his left hand, a six-shooter in the other, and his horse's reins were clenched between his teeth.

It reminded Jonah of that long-ago Saturday afternoon back in Six Bulls country.

With abandon, his uncle came to the bandit bringing up the rear and gunned him out of the saddle.

The next outlaw glanced over his shoulder and spurred his horse to avoid the charging avenger dressed in black.

It was too late, as the big man felled him, too.

Many shots rang out. In the fast-paced action, the stampeding herd of cattle barreled toward the remaining outlaws, as the burros, already bewildered by the noise and confusion, turned around to avoid being trampled. More shots from the hilltops decimated the gang. The leader's horse panicked and bucked him off, throwing him beneath the sharp hooves of the charging cattle.

In a matter of a few minutes, the battle was over.

Standing, Jonah looked across to the next ridge and saw his brother and Alex, who were waving their hats. Gene joined him and said, "I don't think we lost a single man. That was a brilliant plan. Let's go round up the burros with the gold, and then we can catch up to the herd."

All the outlaws were dead, and their bodies remained where they had fallen. Only their guns, saddles, and horses were retrieved.

"The turkey buzzards and coyotes will feed today on their black-hearted gizzards," Captain Renke noted. "It's a fitting end for these murdering gents."

Standing around the campfire that evening, everyone was heady with the success of the day, as Captain Vogel approached carrying several heavy sacks.

"Jonah, you folks did a fine job, and I'm much obliged. This is the reward I promised. I did a rough calculation and figure these sacks hold about five thousand dollars in gold. I'll leave it to you to divide it among your people."

"Thank you, sir. I'm glad the plan worked so well, and we're grateful for the reward. When I get to Yreka, I'll stop in and pay my respects to the mine owner and thank him myself."

"Ah, I'd just as soon you let things ride," Renke replied. "I'll convey your gratitude to Mr. Cort."

"Why is that? We recovered his gold."

"Well, you see the reward was my idea, and of course, I've had no chance to tell him about it. Could be, he'll be a bit touchy on the matter. But, fair is fair. I gave my word, and payment has been made. I'll deal with him, eventually."

"All right, whatever you say. We broke open a keg of whiskey. Help yourself."

"Don't mind if I do," he replied. Filling half of his tin coffee cup and taking a deep sip, he sighed, "Ah, this really hits my sweet spot. Think I'll set a spell. Why don't you Sommer boys join me and fill me in on the happenings in Six Bulls? Frank, you sure take after your mother's fine looks."

"Ma died last year, as the ague swept over the valley, taking her and others in short order. Your kin was spared. And Pa, he recently took himself a new wife."

Renke looked at him. "Well, things change, son. That's the nature of life."

Jonah asked, "Don't you ever miss the land of the Six Bulls?"

"Yep, I think back to the buzzing of the cicadas on warm summer evenings, when the moon was full and bright, and the air was filled with the sweet smell of honeysuckle. And the fine times and adventures your pa and I had on our trip west to start new lives on the prairie." The hardships they had encountered flashed through his mind, and he remembered traveling from Ohio to Missouri and sailing down the big rivers of America on flatboats. "One day, I hope to go back and rest my bones in Six Bulls country. My roots are there, and I'd like to see my kin and friends again. How about you boys, you ever think about going home?"

"Sure," Jonah replied, "I'll go back to visit, but first, I want to see more of California and Oregon."

Renke chuckled and asked, "And how about you, Frank?"

"I'm never going back," the young man said, biting off his words with bitterness. "I have no home there any more."

"Ah, don't go down that road, brother," Jonah chimed in. "Don't pay him no mind, Captain. He's still brooding over events we left behind."

Standing stiffly, Renke nodded. "I'm turning in. It's been a long several days for me, and my backside is aching. See you boys in the morning. And, thanks for the whiskey. You're going to make a lot of miners happy in Yreka with this firewater."

CHAPTER TWENTY-ONE

In a long meadow east of Yreka, the grass was higher than a horse's belly. There, the drovers circled the herd, settling them for the night.

Captain Vogel led one line of the gold-bearing burros, and Frank the other.

"I appreciate the help, Frank," Renke said. "We're close enough to town now that I can drive these animals by myself. I'm much obliged for your help."

"Glad to do it, Uncle."

"Jonah," Renke continued, "I suggest you hold the cattle up here on the grassy plateau. When the word gets out that they're Missouri-and-Arkansas-bred cows to be had on the meadow, I expect there'll be an eager stampede by the miners for back-home beef."

"By golly, I sure hope you're right. We'll need many hungry miners paying a good price for the cattle. We're going to split the herd and drive some to other camps in the area," Jonah replied. "I'd like to be rid of the cows as soon as possible. And I know Mrs. Sparks' drovers will quickly leave when they collect their wages.

Renke nodded. "Some might even take it into their heads to walk off with a few of your cows. I'd have a man posted."

"I'll do that."

"I've got some business up in Grants Pass, and I plan to take the morning stage. I'll likely be gone a couple of weeks. Stay alert, nephew. There are all kinds of men hereabouts, and some are truly cutthroats."

It also crossed his mind that Thorne Cort would not cotton well to the idea of a new competitor for his mercantile store, not to mention the reward money. Waving farewell, he left for Yreka.

His arrival on Main Street caused quite a stir, as he drove the pack animals ahead of him. To his surprise, men began hooraying and clapping, amazed to see him alive and returning with the train of stolen burros.

He stopped the caravan at the company office, where the gold was again stored and guarded, to await the formation of another train. When he was sure everything was in order, he made his way to the Elk Horn Saloon, brushing dust from his clothes.

As he pushed past the swinging doors, good-natured shouts greeted him, and several miners clapped him on the back, congratulating him, as he walked through. Brushing himself off more and removing his black hat, he made it to Cort's table at the rear wall and wearily sat down.

"That was fine work, Captain," the mine owner said, in his deep, gravely voice. "A fellow ran across the string of horses, read the note, and brought the animals to town. The fellow you sent along, we hung him the same day, but first we had a quiet, productive talk with him," the mine owner reported, grinning at his clumsy humor.

"Well, at least my plan worked and you got word about the ambush."

"I sent a large posse to begin tracking you four days ago. Guess I need to send somebody to bring them back."

He heard the words, but he again felt the loss of so many men.

"It's too bad about those men who were killed, but I suppose it couldn't be helped."

Renke Vogel poured himself a drink and looked at the man sitting across from him. "I can see you're not whipping yourself too badly over losing so many."

"Things happen. I learned long ago that a man plays the cards that fate deals him. Afterward, you put it behind you."

He remained silent, savoring the taste of the liquor.

"How many men were in the gang?"

"Over twenty, but that got whittled down to the last dozen."

"How many outlaws got away?"

"None of them will be returning to his thieving ways."

"Tarnation, that was first-rate and must have taken some doing on your part," the mine owner said, in admiration. "You'll find your bonus pouch is a little heavier, Renke. It's my gratitude for a job well done."

Nodding, he refilled both of their glasses.

Cort continued, "I hear that a large herd of cattle is bedded down on the high meadow outside of town. Did you run into those folks on the trail?"

He wasn't surprised at the question, as news traveled fast in a mining camp. "Yep, I ran into them in the middle of nowhere, on the east side of Mount Shasta, so I reckon the Good Lord was looking after me, because I had a lot of luck that morning. The gold could not have been recovered without those cowpunchers throwing in with me. We set up an ambush for the killers and downed every last one of them, with no loss on our side. I'd say it went right well. They're the biggest reason that you have your gold back."

"Where the hell did they come from?"

"Fort Laramie. They were heading for Northern California by way of the Applegate Trail."

"And how did you persuade them to throw in with you?"

"I offered them a reward of five thousand dollars for the recovery of the gold train."

"You did what?"

"Without them, I'd have been outgunned twelve to one. So I did the only sensible thing available to me, I enlisted their help by offering the reward. As I've said, without them, the gold would have been lost forever."

It was obvious that Thorne was having trouble coming to grip with the news that he was now short five thousand dollars. Barely controlling himself, and red-faced with fury, he hissed, "I don't recall approving any such reward?"

"True enough," he replied, "but, then, neither of us expected this vicious attack. As I said, I was fortunate to run across those drovers. And now, you have the rest of your gold back."

"I don't like this one bit," Cort hissed, staring at him. "You get yourself out there right now and tell them that the deal is off. Tell them it wasn't your gold, and that you weren't authorized to offer a reward. Did you hear me? Go on, get out there and tell them, because I'm never going to pay that kind of money."

A thin smile played on Renke's face, as he returned his boss's stare. "Too bad, Mr. Cort, a deal is a deal, and I gave my word to those drovers before the pitched battle began. Besides," he added, "it's water under the bridge, as they've already been paid with refined gold from the train."

The mine owner's face momentarily went blank, and then contorted into a mask of evil fury. "You did what?

Damnation, you can't do that! I never gave you that kind of authority."

Renke poured himself another drink. Lowering his voice, he remarked, "I lost good men out there, trying to fend off the *desperadoes*. And then, I rode all night chasing those outlaws for a hundred miles, into the wildest country imaginable on the far side of Mount Shasta. It was suicide for me to tackle that gang alone, but I wasn't going to give up. Finding those cowpunchers and getting their help was just what I needed. And after all that, you have most of your gold returned." Leaning back in his chair, he added, "No use dwelling on the cards fate deals, just as you said. Best you put it behind you. You know, when the cow kicks over the bucket, you can't pour spilt milk back into a pail."

Thorne's fist slammed the table. "Spilt milk?" he roared, as nearby miners turned to look at them. He lowered his voice, but it was laced with anger. "Is that all you have to say?" Still striving to control himself, he repeated, "Spilt milk! You think my missing money is like spilt milk. Well, Mr. Enforcer, it wasn't your gold, was it? And you're not missing five thousand dollars, are you? Now, you damn well get off your ass and go out there. Let them know that you made a mistake. Give each man a twenty-dollar Gold Eagle and say that they can have a night in the Elk Horn on me—redeye, women, anything. Just get me back the five thousand."

Renke again savored his drink, and returned the mine owner's stare.

"Did you hear me? Why are you sitting there? Get your ass out there or, by heavens, I'll . . ."

"You'll what?" he interrupted forcefully, his eyes blazing. He brought his chair down hard. "I didn't need your urging to follow that gang into the badlands, did I? And you didn't have to tell me that you wanted your gold back, did you?"

"Now, see here, Vogel . . ."

"No, you listen to me! You insisted on me leading the train, didn't you? And why was that? Because you knew I was the best man for the job." Sarcastically, he asked, "You did want the gold recovered, didn't you, boss?" Running his fingers through his long hair, he added, "Sometimes, Cort, you get so caught up in your quest for power and riches that your black heart shines through like a stingy lump of coal."

Cort started to rise from the table, while his right hand dipped into his waistcoat, where he kept his two-shot derringer.

Renke was even faster, drawing his six-gun from its holster. Then, carefully and deliberately, he laid it on the table next to his whiskey glass.

Rethinking his actions, the mine owner sat again, fuming. "If you'd been more on your game, this wouldn't have happened in the first place, you misbegotten, ninnyhammer."

Slowly, Renke stood. With only the table separating them, he intently stared down at the man. In an intimidating voice, he whispered hoarsely, "I'm only going to say this once, Mr. Cort. Never call me names again. Do we understand each other?"

Curbing his temper, the owner snarled, "You're the dealer in this hand, Vogel, but another day will come. Of that, you can be absolutely sure."

"Could be. Now, listen very carefully. If anyone harms those men and the woman who risked their lives to help me, I'm coming straight for you." He put on his hat, while holstering his gun. "I have wages and a bonus coming for my last job. I'd be obliged to have it now."

"You've a lot of nerve, you two-bit, chicken-livered . . ."

"Calm down and let's keep our tempers. And remember to keep a civilized tongue in your head when you talk to me."

"I'll get you for this, Vogel. You can bet on it."

"Maybe." Casually, he looked around, surveying the bustling activity in the saloon, then back at the mine owner. Leaning over the table, he narrowed his eyes and spoke in a low, deep voice, "You have a big operation in Yreka and in this valley, Mr. Cort. You don't need to jeopardize any of it over some little spat between you and me. Now, I'll take what's coming to me."

"I don't like to be threatened, not by you or anyone else, Vogel."

"I made no threats. I'm merely stating the same knowledge that everyone in Yreka has about your business ventures. If any harm comes to those drovers up on the meadow, you'll have to contend with me. Take my advice and put it behind you."

"You realize that you're through in these parts? When I get the word out, you won't be able to find a job anywhere within a hundred miles of this camp."

"I figured as much. I'm only going to ask one last time, pay me what I'm due."

Likely heeding an inner instinct in the tense situation, Cort leaned back, but made sure his hands remained on the table. Then, ever so slowly, using his left hand, he reached into his coat pocket and drew out two pouches of gold dust. His eyes never left the captain, as he carefully pushed the small, leather sacks across the table.

"Thank ye, kindly," Renke said, hefting the bags and pocketing the gold. His gun hand remained loosely at his side, near his bulging holster, as he made his way out of the busy saloon.

———◆———

At his table at the back of the saloon, Cort, fumed with anger and watched the captain walk away, as cheers once more tailed after him, until the man pushed through the swinging doors.

You son of a bitch, you have a lot of nerve, but you're shortsighted in judging me, if you think this matter is over.

Loud shouts momentarily diverted his attention, as the saloon was full of action that evening. Men stood fifteen or more deep in front of the raised stage, where Cort's ladies presented an energetic dance, accompanied by piano and banjo music. They were dressed in colorful outfits, revealing ankles beneath their ruffled skirts and busty proportions. As they sashayed and kicked up their legs, they were only passable performers. Yet, the miners cheered, whooped, and hollered, as though the revealing routine was the real cancan, straight from Paris, France.

Cort turned the last few minutes over in his mind. *No one talks to me that way or deals me out of five thousand dollars,* he thought. Slowly, he calmed down. *There are many ways to get my gold back. If those drovers think otherwise, I'll see that calamity rains down on them. And, if that old man wants to play a knight in shining armor when he returns, he'll get his, too. I run the Sourdough Mine and the Elk Horn, this town, and this valley. That's the way it is, and by damn, it ain't going to change, not for you Vogel, nor for anyone else.*

Smiling thinly, he fingered the elaborate handle of his cane. Pouring himself another drink, he reached for his cigarette fixings.

CHAPTER TWENTY-TWO

The stagecoach trip to Grants Pass took three days. Several times, Renke and the two other male passengers got out to help push the coach up the steeper grades of the trail and over the pass through the Siskiyou Mountains. On the steep down slope, the acrid smell of the stage's smoking wooden brakes, flattened against iron-rimmed wheels, filled the interior of the cabin. The burning smells lingered all the way to the Applegate Tollgate, and finally dissipated once they reached the valley below.

The hot, dusty ride tired him, although he marveled at the beauty of the passing country, viewing it through the stage's small, open window. The mountains rose nearly as tall as the sky, crowned by craggy, sharp edges. Huge, statuesque trees were silhouetted against thickly forested areas, with meadows and lakes dotting the landscape.

The rutted road bounced the coach mercilessly, causing pains to shoot through him with each jolt. His supply of laudanum had long been exhausted, and he looked forward to getting more from Doctor Samuels. *Buck up, me man,* he thought, *this ride won't last forever and then the doc will fix me up. I can't figure out what's causing the trouble in my backside and butt. They say lumbago can hurt folks really bad. Perhaps, that's the issue, or maybe I'm just getting old.* He smiled inwardly at the tired, old joke.

Nostalgically, he recalled his days in Missouri. His lifelong friends and kin were still there, he imagined, although some must have died, like his nephews' mother. His thoughts drifted to his sons and married daughter, and the farms that they had carved out together from the frontier prairie.

When my time comes, I'd like to rest my bones in the land of the Six Bulls. Damnation, the best place would be right there on the land I homesteaded and cleared, where I built my cabin with the veranda porch on all sides, and planted my first crops. By God, those were good days. Well, no sense fussing about it, I'm not going back, not while I'm sufficiently fit.

It surprised him that the trip was so wearing. By the time the driver called out the stop at the booming town of Grants Pass, he was ready for a big steak, a bottle of whiskey, and an early sleep.

The town had grown, sporting more stores on the wide, pot-holed main street. There was vibrancy in the air, and new sawmills, located along the banks of the Rogue River, were the major source. Additionally, droves of migrating settlers were arriving in Oregon, and mining was booming. All this led to rapid growth and an increasing demand for lumber.

Exhausted, Renke ate and went to bed early in a room above the bar and restaurant. The next morning, he set out for the office of Doctor Samuels.

After passing through the door, he cheerily greeted his friend. "Good morning, John. Do you have time to give me another look-over? I've been hurting some, since I last saw you."

"G'day to you, Captain."

"I've been doing a lot of hard trail riding in the past few weeks, Doc, and I figure it's the cause of my discomfort. Maybe you can give me something for my ailments.

"Sure, I can look you over. Go into the next room, and I'll be right with you."

An hour later, he was dressed again.

John Samuels came back to the room and sat on a chair across from him. "Sit down, my friend," he said.

"Well, don't look so glum," Renke replied, trying to lighten the air. "It's just a touch of lumbago. Isn't that right, John? It can't be too bad, as I'm still fit. Let's have it."

"Captain, you have a cancer."

"Oh, how's it treated? You doctors have all your needles, medicines, and book learning. There surely is some way to deal with this thing."

"It is a growth in the body. Nobody really knows where it comes from, or why it spreads. The malignancy kills pieces of a man until the job is finished. It was first identified by the Egyptians, thousands of years ago, and then named by the ancient Greeks.

"From the days of the Romans, doctors believed bloodletting helped. That procedure has not only proven to be false, but it saps the very patients that doctors treat. Sometimes, if the growth is on the skin, I can remove it. Deep-cutting surgery also can be possible, but few survive. The operation tends to be as lethal as the growth, only death comes more quickly.

"There are different types, but yours is generally found among older men. Renke, I'm sorry, but no treatment or cure exists. The only thing that I can do is to try and make you more comfortable, by giving you something for the pain."

Renke stared at his friend, trying to comprehend through a thick veil of denial. "You mean . . . what are you saying, John?"

"You have a tumor and it's malignant. There is nothing anyone can do for you. What you require is more rest, to conserve your strength. Lord knows, you're going to need it. The pain will get worse from here on out. The short of it is that you're dying. The spreading cancer will eventually kill you."

"I thought the reddish-brown stuff you gave me helped. Surely, it does more than just dull the hurt."

"Laudanum is derived from opium," his friend explained. "It only eases your pain, but it won't cure you. And after a while, even it won't be enough to deaden what you'll be feeling."

Grappling with the news, he stared at Samuels. Seeing his friend's serious expression, he acknowledged the truth. "How much longer do you reckon I have, John?"

"Medicine isn't an exact science when it comes to making predictions for this ailment. I'd guess that you have three or four months."

"Sweet Jesus and Mary, Mother of God!"

"I'm sorry, Renke, but you best put your affairs in order."

Shaking his head and in a daze, Renke paid and said goodbye, pocketing the small bottle of painkiller. Without recalling how he got there, he entered the nearest saloon. He spent the next few days in a mindless swirl—carousing, drinking, and attending to the fancy saloon-ladies.

On the morning of the eighth day since leaving Yreka, he awoke with a fearsome headache. Staggering downstairs to breakfast, he began thinking about his future. *I have to get a hold of myself. There're important things that need settling. And, as the Doc Samuels says, time is short.*

I need to check on Jonah and Frank. Who knows, with Cort on his uppity, highfaluting horse, those nephews of mine may have run into trouble. I'm the one who asked for their help, and there's no reason in hell that Thorne should take it out on them. Most likely, though, he'll have some scheme in mind.

Afterwards, I mean to head back to the land of the Six Bulls, and that means a two thousand-mile trip. I can take the stagecoach and steamer to Sacramento, where I can catch another stage. Maybe there's a train these days that can take me part of the way. I'll buy a horse for the last leg of the trip to Seneca. It'll likely take me the better part of two months, más o menos. Traveling home will also allow me to say good-bye to my old friends. But my timing is going to be tight, according to John's estimate.

I best go back and see the doc, again. I'll need enough of his bitter-tasting medicine to see me through to the end. Yep, that's exactly what I'm going to do.

Then, I need to catch the southbound stage and see that the Sommer boys are all right and on their way to a safer place.

CHAPTER TWENTY-THREE

It was late in the afternoon when the stage arrived in Yreka. Renke walked down the main road to the office of the Sourdough Wind Mine, located on the corner of Cort Street. *It isn't enough to have the final say over the whole damn town,* he thought. *This jackass also has to have streets named after himself.*

Entering the building, he startled one of the company clerks.

"Oh, my God, it's you, sir," the young man said, his mouth agape. "We all figured that you lit out for good and were long gone. Mr. Cort has put a price on your head of five thousand dollars. He says you were in cahoots with the outlaw gang that stole his gold, and you made off with a big share of it."

He figured the mine owner would try something, but he didn't reckon on being branded a thief.

The clerk continued, "Cort's had notices posted all over town showing you're a wanted man. And I saw some of his men riding out of town to drive off those cattlemen who came to town with you. They left about twenty minutes ago."

Remaining collected, Renke replied, "Well, I best see him and straighten things out. Where do you suppose he is now?"

"I reckon he's likely at the Elk Horn, sir."

"Much obliged to you for the information."

Turning, he made his way out of the building and quickly walked between two buildings toward the rear of the livery, where he had stabled his horse. He would deal with the mine owner, but right now, his nephews were in danger. His gray horse was eating his oats as he approached. "Hello, big fellow. Sorry to interrupt, but we have a bit of riding to do this evening."

Saddling and mounting, he rode out the back gate and set off for the meadow on the plateau outside of town.

Jonah grimly ducked behind a rock, as another bullet ricocheted off the large rocks in front of him. The gunfire started earlier when he and the others were gathered around the cook fire for supper. Mrs. Sparks and Alex were killed in the first volley. Everyone else scattered, and he, with Frank in tow, made it to the big boulders bordering their camp, only to be pinned down by rifle fire.

Scared, and agitated over the loss of Lisa Annie and Alex, Frank demanded, "Why in the hell are these jackasses shooting at us? If they just wanted to rob us, they could have jumped us, taken our guns, and scattered to the wind. There was no call to gun down those fine folks."

"I don't rightly know, little brother. Just keep your head down. Where did Lem and Gene go?"

"I saw them take cover in those trees to the left," his brother replied, nodding toward the hill.

Jonah took off his hat and very carefully rose, searching for the hidden location of the shooters. Quickly, he ducked, as lead whizzed by, glancing off the big stones behind him. "I saw a gun flash, coming from the bottom of the hill and across the swale in front of us."

"What are we going to do, Jonah? These fellows mean to kill all of us. They've certainly made that clear enough."

"I'm going to try to circle the hill behind them. With us firing from different directions, maybe we can get them to break cover. Then, Lem and Gene will have them in sight."

"There must be seven or eight of them. Watch yourself, big brother."

"And you take care." Crouching low, Jonah made his way to a shallow draw and began the trek, just out of view of the ambushers. *I can't figure out what these fellows are after. Frank is right. They could have gotten the drop on us and taken what's left of the herd, the gold, or perhaps both. He's also right that these fellows are savages with no regard for life. Who else would gun down a man and woman with no warning at all?*

He ran a zigzag course, until he rounded the low hill. Still crouching, he heard gunfire coming from the killers across a creek to his right. Slowly, he moved in that direction. As he came out of a stand of spruce and crossed the shallow creek, he cocked the hammer on his rifle and cautiously stood, seeking a target.

Suddenly, a shooter stood up with his back to him only ten yards away. The man fired his gun across the wetlands at Frank's position, then ducked behind the shelter of a fallen tree.

Jonah partly rose and saw that there was another man sprawled next to the first, who was reloading his gun. Dropping down, he thought, *Bloody hell, I have to deal with these two without alerting the other killers.* Noticing that they fired single-shot, muzzle-loaded rifles, he picked up a good-sized rock and waited until one of them fired his gun, followed in short order by a second shot.

With no time to spare, Jonah was on them, bashing the closest one on the head with the rock. Then, the young man turned to confront the second shooter.

Cornered, the man retreated a few steps and realized there was no time for him to finish reloading. Instead, he grabbed the rifle by the barrel, intent on using it as a lethal club.

Jonah feinted to the right but pulled back at the last instant to avoid the swinging firearm. Then, he rushed in and, using the stock of his rifle, hit the man a mighty blow in the stomach.

With the wind knocked out of him, the man dropped his gun and doubled over.

Instantly, Jonah was on the man, while reaching for his knife, and plunged the blade into the man's heart. Checking the first bandit, he saw him lying on his back. His unseeing eyes were open with the stare of death.

The remaining killers were arrayed in a wide semicircle behind fallen trees, just to his right. He brought his gun to bear and suddenly stopped at the sound of rapidly approaching hoofbeats.

Rounding a bend to his right, Captain Vogel's gray stallion moved like a banshee shot from a canon. Atop, the big man's black hat flew off, his white hair streaming behind. He held a pistol in one hand and a rifle in the other. Between his teeth, he held the horse's reins, just like the fight with the gold-train outlaws.

Jonah stood, open-mouthed and dumbfounded at the imposing sight of his uncle, riding low in the saddle and hell-bent straight for the killers. He quickly calculated that his uncle was heading into a trap. *My God, when those fellows see him, they'll cut him down with their guns. I have to* distract them. Thinking fast, he ran for the cover of large boulders twenty yards to his left. When he was half way there, he bellowed his Indian call loudly, *"Yeooowee,"* and fired his gun in the general direction of the outlaws.

They turned toward him and return his gunfire. As he dove behind the large stones, bullets thudded and ricocheted in all directions, one ripping the hat off his head.

In the next instant, his uncle thundered into the shooters. His horse ran over the closest man, and he downed another with a pistol shot.

The last four skedaddled for their horses, with the captain in close pursuit. As they broke cover from behind the rocks, rifle shots from Lem, Gene, and Frank ended the battle.

Jonah stood and hurried to the captain. "Uncle, that grand entrance you made was risky, but it wasn't a moment too soon for us."

Renke looked at him, while controlling his skittish horse. Dryly, he commented, "Much obliged, nephew. That was quick thinking on your part, distracting these varmints. You got lots of grit." He dismounted and turned over the two dead men. "Just as I figured. These are Cort's men."

The others joined them.

Lem had a tear in his eye, as he turned over one of the killers. Wiping his nose on the back of his sleeve, he said, "We were about to sit and have our supper, Captain, when these cowards opened fire. There was no 'howdy' or any warning, and Mrs. Sparks and Alex were gunned down in the first volley. What in the hell is going on hereabouts? This Yreka territory has turned out to be mighty unfriendly."

Captain Vogel remained silent.

"If that don't beat all," Jonah continued. "They could have given a shout-out for us to surrender and throw down our guns. Instead, they killed two fine folks outright. What kind of low-life savages does such killing? "

"Were they after the cows?" Frank asked, shocked at the sight of the dead men. "More likely, they knew about the gold from the reward. I expect that was the reason."

"And why did they mark us for killing?" Lem added. "Like Jonah says, they could have snuck up and robbed us, taken our guns and horses, and rode away, free as birds."

"Uh-huh, that's what I wonder," Lem added.

The captain's face was set in a fearsome expression. In a voice filled with emotion, he began, "There's payment to be demanded for these killings. And only one fellow in this valley means you folks harm. I guess I knew it in my bones. Even so, I had no inkling that his vengeance would turn to cold-blooded murder. It's my fault. I shoulder the blame for the loss of Alex and Mrs. Sparks. I traveled for personal reasons up to Grants Pass, and that left you folks exposed."

Taken aback, Frank was the first to speak. "Uncle, you didn't pull the trigger on Mrs. Sparks or Alex. In fact, you saved our hides by surprising those mangy mongrels the way you did. The blame lies somewhere else."

"He's right," Jonah added.

There were murmurings of agreement from the other two.

The captain turned over the last killer. "Most of these men used to work for me," he said. "And I worked for Thorne Cort, the high-muck-a-muck, as the Chinese laborers say, that owns the Sourdough Wind Mine and Elk Horn Saloon. I knew that he was more furious than a hornet's nest at my paying out the reward money to you men, but I never figured it'd come to this."

"This Cort must be one bad *hombre*," Lem commented.

"That man likely thinks I crossed him," his uncle added. "You may not be aware, but he also owns the mercantile in town. He's an arrogant scoundrel who never did cotton to having competitors. The merchandise you hauled in your wagons, and your Missouri cows, must have cut into his business and made him even more agitated. Then, when I left town, he probably figured he had a free rein to deal with you folks."

"That man is a low-life and not worthy of walking the streets of Yreka or any other place," Jonah said, a hard edge to his voice.

"You got that right, nephew," his uncle agreed. "This region is going to become really treacherous for all of us, come morning. I suggest you men take what's left of your herd and head north to the most-recent gold strike, up Oregon way in Jacksonville, on Rich Gulch Creek. When I was in Grants Pass, everyone was talking about the big gold finds there."

"It sounds like the right place for us to go," Lem agreed. "Let's hope they're more welcoming in Oregon than the folks are here in California."

"Maybe Oregon is a good suggestion," Jonah added, his voice full of emotion, "but I'm not leaving until the record is set right in this valley. They might have done us all in, if you hadn't shown up. As it is, there's a score to settle for Alex and Mrs. Sparks."

"Best you look to yourselves and head north," Renke replied. "I'll take care of the mine owner in town."

"That varmint is the cause," Jonah replied, "and I need to scratch my itch for justice. I ain't one to tuck tail and run. Besides, you're going to need my help. There'll be too many of them for one man to handle."

His uncle nodded. "I see your point."

"I'm coming along," Frank chimed up. "It's just as much my fight as it is yours, Uncle Renke."

The captain looked at his nephew. "I reckon that's so. I have something in mind that'll accommodate you, Frank, as well as Lem and Gene, if you fellows are willing to help."

Jonah added, "A rancher up the valley has offered to buy most of the herd for breeding stock, and he's offered a good price. That'd leave us with about a hundred cows. We have a couple of hours of daylight left. Lem, you and Gene get the herd headed north. Frank, you complete the sale with the rancher and then keep the herd moving."

Frank started to complain, "Looki here, brother . . ."

"Little brother, if we're going to get out of this valley alive, we need to move the herd and sell what we can to the rancher. That's important to all of us, and I need you to get it done."

"Frank," Renke chimed in, "hold your breeches up and listen for a moment. I have a plan in mind that'll hit Cort's operations hard, right where it'll hurt him the most, in his money belt. As you fellows drive the cows north, you can do the damage before you meet with the rancher. How about giving me a listen?"

The younger man looked from Jonah to the captain. "All right, it seems like the choice has been made for me. First, we have some burying to do."

"No need dealing with the killers, the coyotes can clean up this mess, just as they did with the murderers we met on the trail," Renke remarked.

As the shadows lengthened, the men stood silently over the two freshly dug graves of their friends, hats in hand.

Jonah looked at his uncle, who nodded to him. The young man stepped forward and began to pray.

"Lord, the miseries for Lisa Annie Sparks are now over. She came a long way to get to this valley, even sailed across the sea. Keep her with you, oh Lord, and comfort her, now that she can be united with her husband, James.

"I didn't know Alex for very long, but he didn't deserve to die this way. He served in the army and

was mighty helpful in getting us here with the herd. I'll be calling on you to look after him, too, Lord. That's about all I have to say.

Amen."

Somberly, the men hitched the teams, broke camp, and split into two groups, intent on rendering justice.

CHAPTER TWENTY-FOUR

Frank rode point, leading the herd across the grasslands, with forested mountains to his right and high peaks to his left. After traveling north for several miles, he searched for the area that his uncle had described.

After rounding a knoll, he spotted the flume about a quarter of a mile away, angling across the bluff, just as the captain had said. The aqueduct crossed over swales and hillsides, funneling water to meet the hungry energy needs of the Sourdough mining operation. It was one place where the waterway was readily accessible from the floor of the broad valley.

Gene remained with the herd as Frank and Lem approached the structure. The sound of the swift-moving water was like a furious whisper above the stamping mill's angry noise, which drifted up the valley from miles away. Thick pole logs, with their ends planted into the ground, supported the spindly looking structure. Their plan was to shut down both the mine and the mill by tearing away this part of the waterway.

"This looks like a place for us to do our work, Lem," the young man observed. "We can easily climb up to the planked watercourse."

"Uh-huh, let's separate our horses by thirty or forty yards, loop our lariats around the elevated trough, and see what happens when the animals take up the slack. We'll have to mind your uncle's words of caution to avoid the falling structure and the torrent of water that'll be dumped on us. If it starts to move, unwind the rope from your saddle horn and get, fast."

Minuets later, Frank shouted, "My line is set. Are you about ready, Lem?"

"Yep. On my mark, we'll pull together. Three, two, one and go."

Each horse took up the strain.

"Ya-ha, get up and pull, you doggone excuse for a pony," Frank yelled, slapping the animal's haunches with his hat and using his spurs.

Frank heard the creaking of wood under stress, then a terrible screeching noise. Looking back, the structure remained unmoved.

Riding toward the young man, Lem noted, "In addition to the large support pilings, the weight of the water makes it very heavy, so it's hard to dislodge. We're going to need more animals to move this damn thing. Best we go back for the mules."

A half-hour later, they returned with Gene and the eighteen mules. The men set about hitching the animals in tandem, deciding to apply all the pulling power at one point of the waterway.

Gene seemed intimidated by the sheer size of the wooden structure and the huge quantity of water that sloshed down the plank-sided waterway. "Fellows," he observed, "we may be successful dislodging a section, but then we're going to have to run like hell to avoid being drowned."

Lem stroked his beard, as he mulled their options. "Gents, if we tie all our ropes together, we should have nigh onto a hundred-fifty feet. We'll slip one end around the planks and then attach the other to the harnessed mules. Gene, you have that really sharp ax. You stand by with your horse, and when that damn thing starts to tilt, chop the rope and quickly head for the herd."

"Let me do it," Frank volunteered. "You fellows deal with the animals and leave the cutting to me. Hand me the ax, Gene."

They spent time getting the harnessed teams aligned in tandem and splicing the single line. When all was set, Gene mounted the lead mule, while Lem rode back to Frank.

"You ready, young man?"

"I think so."

Lem took out his pistol, raised it in the air and fired, startling the mules into action. Galloping to the head of the line, he yelled loudly, "Yee-haw, get your backs into it and pull, you misbegotten, four-legged critters."

Immediately, Gene kicked his mule into action. The rope literally hummed, as it snapped taut.

"Ha, yip, yip, get your asses moving," Lem shouted.

Frank watched the structure and heard the wood groan, followed by high screeches. *How in blue blazes will I know when the time is right to sever the rope? Too soon, and we have to start again. If I'm late, I'll be swamped.*

More sounds of stress came from the waterway, and water began lapping over the plank sides.

Suddenly, a plank section parted, sending a huge geyser arching through the air, which landed twenty yards from Frank. Simultaneously, the collapsing waterway's skeletal frame whipped the rope in a new direction, again snapping it taut, which caught Frank across the forehead and bowled him over.

Lem saw the accident, and galloped back to help. The flow of water was swiftly moving toward the fallen young man, as the high-pressure water plume gyrated and writhed snake-like.

Frank moaned and slowly turned over on the ground, obviously stunned.

Leaping from his horse, the old prospector grabbed Frank by the collar and helped him stand.

He was stunned, and a bright-red rope bruise creased his forehead.

"C'mon, Frank, get your wits about you. We have to get on with it, so give me the ax. You climb on your horse and ride to the herd."

He looked at the waterway and couldn't believe his eyes. The flume was at an odd angle and tipping toward them. Struggling, he clambered astride his horse. "Lem, it's going to give way any moment. Let's go," he screamed.

Swinging a mighty blow, Lem brought the ax down on the rope and hurriedly turned to mount his horse.

Unbelievably, half of the line remained intact.

For a moment, both men stared in amazement.

Then, quicker than the blink of the eye, more strands began unfurling and snapping until, explosively the rope ends flew in opposite directions.

With the tension suddenly released, most of the mules stumbled to their knees. Struggling to regain their footing, Gene used his whip to get the long string of animals moving quickly toward the distant herd and safety.

Laboring, Lem mounted his horse. "Hell's fire, ride, boy, ride like the devil himself is chasing you, because he is."

Loud crashing sounds came from the framed structure, as the two men rode for their lives. The original geyser became a crescendo of cascading water, moving about like a gyrating cyclone.

Joining Gene, the three looked in amazement toward the hillside. Unbelievably, the waterspout's destructive force scoured hillsides, carrying away scaffolding and support beams, as more sections of the structure collapsed, one after another.

"It's falling over like a line of dominoes," Lem observed.

Frank was still unsteady, but he added, "Perhaps it's a reminder from the Almighty, smiting the evil man's mining operation with his swinging sword of redemption?"

"Someone better turn off the water," Gene wryly commented.

They stared in awe at the newly crated cascade, as it finally found a route to a dry gulch, which began carrying the flood tide toward a distant river. Only then did the beam and plank flume stop collapsing.

Continuing to stare at the destruction, Frank said excitedly, "Listen! Do you fellows hear anything besides the pouring water?"

"I hear nothing," Gene replied, "except the cattle bawling."

"That's exactly the point," Lem added, with gusto. "The mine owner's crusher has been plumb discombobulated into silence."

With a wide grin, Frank said, "Let's ride. We'd better reach that rancher before we lose every bit of daylight."

CHAPTER TWENTY-FIVE

Captain Renke Vogel walked his horse in the lengthening shadows of early evening, with Jonah trailing behind. Whale oil lanterns, hung on posts, lit the town's main street, as miners went about their evening pursuits.

Remaining on the backside of the buildings fronting the street, Renke led the way to the rear of the livery stable without drawing attention. He whispered, "Cort will have men out looking for me, as he's surely gotten word that I'm back in Yreka. When Frank and the boys disable the stamping mill, he'll want to know why. Most likely, he'll send some of his men to find out what happened and to make repairs. Those fellows will get right on it, but it'll take time to organize, hitch the teams, and load wagons. Let's stay here until then, and we can watch the whole thing from the loft."

"What happens afterwards," Jonah asked.

"I'll slip into the Elk Horn from the rear. I know its layout well. You stay with the horses and be ready to ride."

"What about you and . . ."

"Shhh, listen," he interrupted, holding up his hand. Except for the lively sounds coming from the street and saloons, there was a strange stillness. The jarring, ever-present pounding of the stamping mill was missing. "They've done it, Jonah! They've managed to bring down the flume. Now, Cort's entire mining operation has come to a halt. That'll make the turkey buzzard take notice. Let's keep a watch on the front doors of the saloon."

Soon, a group of men scurried out the swinging, bat-like doors.

"Those are his men," Renke whispered. "Nine, as I count them."

In short order, three horse-drawn wagons sped out of town, accompanied by a dozen riders.

"They picked up a few more gents," Renke noted. "That's good. It leaves him with only a few remaining in town. Actually, fixing the waterway is likely to be a big job. First, they'll have to ride to Humbug Creek, about ten miles north of town, and open the alternate channel to divert the water away from the flume. Only then can they begin the repairs. It'll likely take them many days to get the job done.

"I'm going to pay my old boss a visit and put a torch to the saloon. When you see it blazing, you get on your horse and ride out of Yreka, quick-like."

"I won't leave without you."

Renke saw the worried look on his nephew's face. "Don't you understand me? Your life will depend on you leaving. The fire will also mean that I'll be departing as fast as I can. If there're no flames in the next ten minutes, you'll know that I failed. Then, leave and join your brother up north."

"How are you going to get away? Everyone in town knows you."

"True enough, but not everyone is willing to cross my path," he replied simply.

"God be with you, Uncle."

"Good fortune to us both."

Renke made his way along the back of the buildings fronting Main Street, until he reached the rear door of the barroom. Quickly, he slipped inside. Shielded by a heavy drape, he surveyed the room carefully from his darkened viewpoint.

Excited miners gathered around the gaming tables. Men standing next to the roulette wheel shouted eagerly, calling out their favorite numbers. The air was thick with tobacco smoke that hovered near the ceiling, as though a heavy fog had settled over the large room. He saw Cort sitting and smoking one of his elaborately crafted cigarettes at his rear table. A man sat across the table from him with his back to Renke.

All the overhead lanterns blazed brightly, accented by the lighted wall sconces. Everything seemed normal.

Making his way in the dark through an adjoining storeroom, Renke circled to the backside of the main room and peered again. Now, Cort sat with his back to him, and, sitting on the other side, was Steinke, a gunman on the mine owner's payroll.

He saw his former boss looking over the crowd nervously. *Cort's wondering why his crusher is shut down. Maybe, he's even worried. Ain't that a shame?* He unhooked the leather thong holding his pistol's hammer and moved the gun up and down in the holster twice, making sure it slid smoothly. Adjusting his hat, he stepped out of the dark and into the brightly lit room.

Steinke immediately saw him and half-stood, while simultaneously pushing back his chair with one leg and drawing his gun. The awkward moves cost him a split-second of time and his life, as Renke's Colt roared.

The man fell sideways, sprawled in a heap, as gun smoke spiraled toward the ceiling.

Instantly, the large room went silent, as all eyes turned toward Renke and the mine owner.

"Evening, Cort," he said, icily.

The gun action momentarily puzzled the mine owner, until he turned in his seat and saw the enforcer. "Vogel, welcome back," he said, with a false bravado. "I don't know why Steinke went for his pistol. There must be some kind of a mix-up here."

"I understand you wanted to see me," Renke answered. "In fact, you wanted it so bad that you put a price on my head, and we both know that's why Steinke drew his gun. And just so there are no accidents, use the side of your arm and send that bloody cane to the floor. Then, very gently, do the same with the dainty little gun from you vest pocket and toss it, too. Careful, take it slow, and do as I say."

Complying, both weapons clattered to the floor. In a harsh, gravelly voice, Cort demanded, "You don't hear the stamping mill, do you? I'm asking you straight out, is that some of your handiwork?"

Pushing back his hat, Renke returned the mine owner's gaze.

A deep flush evidencing his anger, the Sourdough owner grumbled, "I see. You've really gone off the deep end this time, Vogel. Let me make something very clear to you. This is my town, and you no longer have any place hereabouts. Get out, while you're still able."

"That's downright unfriendly, but it's also not a problem. You see, I've a place way back in the hills," Renke lied, "and I reckon it's time for me to take things easier. Before I leave, you have to be brought to account for the killings you ordered today. Truth has a power all its own, Mr. Cort."

"Go to hell, you dumb jackass. You'll never get a job around here again. You know that, don't you?"

Ignoring the mine owner, Renke addressed the crowded room once more. "All of you, hear me! This evening, Cort's men ambushed the drovers up on the meadow who sold the merchandise and Missouri beef that most of you have been enjoying. I take no pleasure in telling you that they killed a woman and a former army man tonight. Those folks had no warning and no chance to defend themselves. I'm here to exact justice for the killing of those innocents."

You'll never get away with this," Thorne whispered in anger.

"And you," Renke spoke in a loud voice, addressing his former boss, "I told you once to leave those cowpunchers alone. Like you often do, you hear only what you want."

"You can't tell me what to do, not in my saloon and not in my town. Now get the hell out of here!" the mine owner shouted.

Ignoring him, the captain turned toward the crowd again. In his booming, authoritative voice, he commanded, "The Elk Horn Saloon is closed. Make your way out the front doors.

Men looked at him, perhaps thinking that this was some kind of stunt. Some walked out, but most seemed frozen in place. Still, the fancy women immediately melted away.

Renke waited for only a moment before he gruffly ordered, "Limber up and move out! AND DO IT NOW!"

Suddenly, there was a mad departure, as miners jostled one another and squeezed through the bar doors. Chairs and tables were turned over and spittoons spilled. In mere moments, the building was empty. Near the ceiling, tobacco smoke swirled about, agitated by the rush through the doors.

Blustering, Cort stormed, "You did me out of my gold, and by damn, I'm going to get it back. You can't storm in here and shoot up my place. Now, I'll add the legal charge of you willfully gunning down Steinke. You know the kind of muscle I have in Yreka. Hell, when I'm done, you'll either be bleeding from a dozen holes, or swinging in a tree, with the birds pecking out your eyeballs."

"That'll be the day."

"You can count on it 'Mr. Ex-enforcer.' Now, get out of my saloon and go straight to hell. My men will be all over you in short order, and you know it. I figure you've gone plumb crazy."

"Uh-huh. You talk too damn much, and that really irks most everybody that knows you."

"When I get through with you, Vogel, your neck is going to have a strange-looking crook from the hangman's noose."

"You do need to learn better manners, you dirty, ring-tailed, crooked scoundrel. Those folks your men killed up in the meadow, they never did any dirt to you. In fact, without their help, your gold would be long gone." Looking around the saloon, he continued, "There's little doubt that I have a day of reckoning coming to me for many of my deeds."

"You can bet on it."

"But you, Mr. Cort, you also have to pay for your vile actions. Most folks call it justice, and that time begins right now."

Renke scanned the room while keeping a wary eye on the owner. "This saloon is another moneymaking gold mine for you, isn't it? You cheat the miners with rigged games, and you water down the whiskey. Well, I might as well get on with what I came to do."

"What in damnation are you yammering about, you overgrown, ancient jackass? Get your ass out of here right now, and could be I'll forget that we had this little talk."

"Sure, and the moon is nothing but a big round of cheese," Renke replied, disdainfully. He moved backward along the rear wall, his right hand hovering over the pistol holster, as he watched Cort. At the first whale oil sconce, he blindly felt with his other hand and grabbed the back of a chair. Lifting it swiftly, he swung it high and smashed the light fixture on the wall.

Instantly, flaming whale oil streamed down and flowed along the planked floor like an evil serpent, consuming the sawdust, while long tongues of flames licked the base of the wall.

Alarmed, Thorne shouted, "Stop this madness right now! How in the hell do you think that you'll get away with this mindless act? You really have gone out of your mind. Do you hear me? Stop it!"

Moving fast, Renke shattered a second wall lamp and then a third. "You do need a hard lesson, Mr. Cort," he roared, as flames licked along the entire wall. "And nothing seems to hurt you as much as losing money, and that cuts you to the quick."

The mine owner stood and backed away from the leaping flames. Pretending to stumble, he turned his back to his ex-enforcer and went down on his knees. Picking up his two-shot, over-and-under derringer, he turned and aimed the gun.

Even quicker, Renke fired, hitting the mine owner in the upper arm.

Cort's small pistol dropped to the floor, as the force of the bullet knocked him to the floor. Desperately grasping his cane, he cradled and leveled the lethal point, then pulled the trigger.

The bullet hit Renke in the arm, knocking him on his backside. He recovered quickly, as the fire raged about him. With his gun hanging down in one hand, he made his way through the smoke and grabbed Cort's coat collar with the other. He dragged the man across the room, out the swinging bat-doors, and deposited him in a mud puddle in the middle of the main street.

The flames leaped higher, as one lamp after another crashed down, adding more fuel to the roaring blaze. The rapidly moving events sent a wave of panic through the town. Some fled the increasingly raging inferno, while many formed bucket brigades, bringing water from the creek to the fire, hoping to contain it. The effort proved to be futile, as the flames leaped to the building adjoining the Elk Horn.

Cort and Renke remained in the middle of the dirt road, ignored and almost lost in their own small world.

"You damn, stinking piece of trash," the Sourdough owner snarled.

"It's funny how things happen, Thorne. What goes around comes back to bite you in the ass. And stop whining like a braying mule and stay put." A movement across the road caught his eye. He saw a shadow toss a lit street lantern through the storefront window, then a second. Recognizing the figure, he hurried to the boardwalk and urgently said, "Jonah, get thee gone."

"I couldn't let such a beautiful opportunity for justice go to waste," the young man replied, with a wicked smile.

"Fine, now head back to the stable."

Returning, Renke stood over the owner, still lying in the mud. The glow of the hot, raging flames lit the mine owner's face as the two men glowered at each other.

Cort groaned, "Not the store, too, you bastard. You've already taken down my other ventures."

"I'm glad you reminded me, Mr. Cort, as there is one last thing. You're going to be personally responsible for anything else that happens to any of those drovers. Do you get my meaning?"

Holding a handkerchief against his wounded arm, the mine owner stared at him, malice and hate twisting his features into a mask of evil, highlighted by the bright glow of the raging fires.

"Understand!"

"I reckon."

"I can't hear you."

"Yes," Cort replied in a loud growl, "I understand."

Turning, Renke walked away, straight through the crowd of scurrying men, his gun hand still hanging down. Jonah was inside the stable, holding the reins of both horses. "Damn, why aren't you already gone, son? Here, tie this bandana around my arm to stop the bleeding from this scratch. I think it's time we left Yreka, and pronto."

The two mounted and galloped out of the building and onto the main road.

Two of Cort's men were helping him stand, and they saw the fast-approaching riders. "There they are," a voice shouted. "Gun them down."

"Give me that pistol," Cort snarled. Resting the barrel on his forearm, he took aim and fired.

Ducking, Renke ran his horse toward the group, scattering them. "C'mon, Jonah, ride like the wind and keep your butt low in the saddle," he shouted.

Bent over the neck of his horse, Renke galloped around the corner of a building and out of town. Slowing, he looked back at Jonah, shouting, "Yip-yip-hurrah, we surely did a good night's work, Jonah."

His smile faded as he saw his young nephew leaning to one side, holding his leg. Coming alongside he asked, "Where are you hit?"

"I took a bullet in my leg."

Riding side-by-side, he made sure his nephew stayed in his saddle. No question, Thorne's men would ride after them in short order. He steered the horses through a stand of evergreens beyond the edge of town. The trees' long, lacy skirts touched the ground, providing a thicket for them to hide temporarily. Tying the reins, he helped Jonah off his horse and sat him on the ground.

In the dim evening light, Renke saw the blood gushing from the jagged wound. Quickly, he stripped off the young man's belt and tied it around the leg to stem the flow. Untying Jonah's neckerchief, he pressed it hard against the leg. "Son, you'll have to keep pressure on it until we can get the lead out."

The sound of approaching horses caught his attention. Through the filigree of low-hanging limbs, he watched the gang of men sweep by in the last light of day. "Take it easy, boy, them fellows are on a wild goose chase. It's already too dark to track us. That bunch is wildly riding about the countryside, so they can report to Cort that they made an effort."

He took an extra shirt from his saddlebag and tore it into strips, wrapping them around the young man's wound. "I have to get you back to the others, then we can deal with your leg. The bleeding will dwindle, but we need to travel slow-like."

"I saw him, Captain."

"Who?"

"I saw the mine owner shoot at us, as we left town."

"I know, son, I saw him, too. That man never will learn to use his ears, but that's all right. We've done him real hurt in all his moneymaking businesses. But it leaves me with one last task."

CHAPTER TWENTY-SIX

"Hello, the camp," Renke called, silhouetted in the darkness against the red glow of the sky behind him, as the fire in town continued to spread.

"Who goes there," Frank challenged.

"It's your uncle." He walked his horse near the campfire, holding onto the reins of Jonah's horse.

"Where is Jonah?" Only then did Frank see his brother slumped over. "Oh, my God, it's Jonah. Captain, tell me he's just hurt and not dead."

Dismounting, he explained, "He took a bullet in the leg as we were leaving town. I have to get it out. Let's lay him down near the fire for the best light."

Lem helped him ease Jonah to the ground.

Frank was beside himself with worry. "It's all my fault for running away from Pa's farm in Missouri. If I hadn't insisted, Jonah wouldn't be lying here on the ground. My God, what have I done?" he cried, sobbing over his brother.

"Hey, boy, get a grip. I need to fish that bullet out, and your wailing doesn't make it any easier."

"Sorry, Uncle Renke. What can I do?'

"I'll need two knives, so lend me yours, Frank. And here, stick my blade deep in the coals of the fire. Lem, find me a jug of whiskey."

"You want me to stick your knife in the fire? What are you going to do with it? Why do you need two knives? What about Jonah and . . ."

"Stop your yammering and do as I say!"

"Yes, sir."

Cutting away the pant leg, Renke exposed the wound. "Here, Jonah, take a swig and then bite down on this stick."

Still agitated, Frank began," I don't understand . . ."

Interrupting the young man, Renke said in exasperation, "Boy, either pull yourself together or go stand beyond the wagons. There isn't time for this nonsense. I need to tend to your brother." He poured whiskey over the knife, cleansing it. "Gene and Lem, hold him down." Prodding the wound for the ball, he made three cuts and fished it out.

Jonah thrashed about in pain, deeply sinking his teeth into the wood.

"I removed it, but the wound needs to be closed. Frank, can you hand me my knife from the fire." Looking at Jonah, he said, "I'm sorry, this has to be done." Immediately, he held the red-hot blade to the wound, searing it, as the smell of burning flesh filled the air.

"Fortunately, our young leader is out cold," Lem said.

"Good. What he needs now is rest. Best we all get some, for tomorrow is shaping up to be another long day."

At first light, they ate a cold breakfast of biscuits and beans and then broke camp. Jonah was awake in the bed of a wagon and resting on a pallet of blankets.

With his arm properly bandaged, Renke approached him. "You're looking better, and you don't look to have much of a fever. You're going to be fine, but you have to stay off that leg until the wound heals. Fortunately, the bullet missed the bone. Frank," he called out, "come look after your brother."

"You're going after the mine owner again, aren't you?" Jonah asked, gritting his teeth.

"Could be."

"You're going to need help."

"I can ride with you," Frank offered, as he approached and heard the conversation.

"Thank you for your offer, but I won't need any help this time. Besides, I can't take any more chances of losing you boys. Your pa would skin me alive. And you, Jonah, you've already acquired two wounds from your tussles that you'll carry around for the rest of your life."

Something in his uncle's words caused Jonah to look at him. "You are coming with us, aren't you, Uncle?"

"No, boys, I've decided to return to the land of the Six Bulls."

Shocked at the disclosure, Frank stammered, "I know we've been a passel of trouble for you, Uncle Renke, but I sure wish that you'd go north with us."

Jonah added, "You can't just up and leave. I kind of figured that we'd all go in on a spread in Oregon."

"You love the West," Frank added. "You told us that many times on the trail."

"Well, things change, and that's the way it is, nephews. I'm going south to catch the steamboat for Sacramento. Then, I'm returning to Missouri. I'm sorry to disappoint you fellows, but I have no choice. You boys can return to Missouri some day and regale your folks with the tales of your many adventures on the western frontier."

"There's nothing in Missouri for me any more," Frank replied. "I'm never going back to Six Bulls country."

Renke looked at him for a moment and answered simply. "I'm sorry you feel that way. Even good people get it wrong at times."

Propping himself up by holding onto the side of the wagon, Jonah said, "You haven't told us why you're leaving so suddenly for Missouri."

"Years ago, I caused my kinfolk deep pain, so I left Six Bulls country," Captain Renke replied. "I wanted to let that wound heal." Chuckling, he added, "A man can't ride a horse much farther west than Yreka to get away from Missouri. Now, I have a hankering to see the old homestead again, and I want Six Bulls to be the final resting place for my weary bones. You see, boys, I have a cancer and the doc up in Grants Pass says that I don't have much time left."

Frank was stunned. "You're dying? There must be something that they can do for you."

"Not this time."

Jonah shook his head in disbelief.

"You're both men now," Renke continued, "and you're in the wilds of the western frontier. Bad things can happen here, but it's also a land where a man can make his mark and set down roots. No sense either of you blistering yourselves over what might have been. Life is short, so make sure you live yours fully. I'm right proud to have you as kin."

Somberly, Jonah nodded. "But, you are going to hit Cort's operations again, aren't you?"

"Could be that I'll see what I can do to make his life difficult on my way south." He turned to his young nephew. "Before I leave, Frank, I have a question for you. Don't you have anything that you want me to pass along to your relatives?"

"I've already said my piece. I have no home in Missouri and no family, not any more. After we dispose of the herd, I'm going to see more of this big land. It might be that I'll get myself up to Washington Territory and stake out a claim up there. I don't know what else to say because my head is fogged with the news of you leaving us."

Jonah searched in his coat, then gave up. "A gold nugget is in my pocket, sir, which I'd like you to give to my pa. Would you please pull it out for me?"

Complying, he placed it in the boy's hand.

"Thanks. Tell him I'll return for a visit to the farm some day after I see more of the West. And give him this nugget. Will you do that for me, Uncle Renke?"

"I'll make a point of it, Jonah. And Frank, are you sure you have no message that you want me to carry back?"

"I've already said my piece, sir."

Turning toward Lem, Renke continued, "Lem, take these boys under your wing for a spell and get yourselves off to Jacksonville. All of you have a deep poke from the reward and your sales, so go ahead and live high on the hog, but do it up Oregon way."

"Reckon we can get most of these animals over the mountains," Lem replied. "It's too early for the pass to be snowed in. I'll watch over the boys for a time." The old miner stepped closer, and the two men shook hands. "I'm mighty glad to have made your acquaintance, Captain Vogel."

"Well, God bless and keep yourselves safe," Renke said to his nephews. Looking toward Lem and Gene, he touched the brim of his hat and mounted, then turned his horse south and called out, "*Vaya con Dios.*"

Jonah watched his uncle disappear around the base of a hill. "There goes a legend, riding to catch the steamboat for home."

"...and heading off to rest his bones in Missouri."

"...in the land of the Six Bulls."

Pausing for a moment, Frank wondered aloud, "What do you think he has in mind for Thorne Cort?" Smiling, he added, "I'll wager it's really going to be something. I sure wish we were going with him. Don't you, Jonah?"

"You got that right."

Choices

CHAPTER TWENTY-SEVEN

New Philadelphia

In her room, Eva anxiously opened the latest letter from Frank. It had been many weeks since his last one, and she found herself fretting and worrying. Her sister had asked more than once about any recent news, which was awkward for her to handle. She tried to calm herself by breathing deeply, but felt aflutter, as butterflies churned in her stomach. With trembling hands, she began reading.

December 3, 1888

My dearest Eva,

I don't know why your last letter took so long to reach me, but each one brings me hope and happiness. I am sorry that your library meeting upset you so. There will always be people who take advantage of the good work that others do. You make me very happy, knowing that our rough patch is behind us. And I take heart that my proposal remains in your thoughts.

We had snow yesterday, and it came after I went into the woods and cut myself a Christmas tree. It is tall, but the cabin accommodates it well, and I love the smell of pine indoors. I decorated it with small pinecones and an angel I bought in town from a wood carver. And, I have boughs of mistletoe hanging from one of the beams. I long to have you here beside me, helping me prepare for the holiday. When that time comes, we will watch the falling snow through the windows, warmed by the burning logs in the fireplace. I hope it is next Christmas. What do you think?

I would like to finish my traveling story, which brought me here to live on the Wallace River. That way, you will know me fully. I do not want there to be any surprises between us.

North of Yreka, we kept the herd headed to Jacksonville. It was early summer, and it rained hard, but we slogged our way through. The Applegate Toll Road over the Siskiyou Pass was private, and we haggled a bit over the toll charge. We finally settled by leaving two cows. During the journey, Jonah regained his strength and the wound healed.

We did a brisk business selling the remaining cattle in Jacksonville. That mining camp was rougher than Yreka. Even so, there were similarities. Gene and I got jobs working in a gold mine located right under the town, while Jonah set out to find land that he could claim and farm. Congress had passed the Donation Land Claim Act in 1850, which expired at the end of 1855. Its intent was to promote land ownership

in Oregon. One hundred-sixty acres were granted
to every unmarried citizen eighteen years or older
who filed a claim. If you were married, the acreage
doubled. Jonah was committed to finding his land
and he did. It lies east of Jacksonville, over the hills
in a valley bordering the Applegate River. It's a small
world, as his neighbor is the same Lindsay Applegate
who owned the toll road through the mountains.

From passing travelers, we eventually learned what
Uncle Renke's departing message was to the owner of
the Sourdough Wind Mine. Even though the store and
saloon were destroyed, among many others, and the
mining operation was without power, he thought of a
final way to deliver justice, and it had to do with the
water provided by Humbug Creek.

A wing dam diverted water from the creek to the
flume. One way to fix the damaged waterway was to
wait for the dry season. Such a delay did not suit Mr.
Cort, as that would leave most of his mining operation
idle until the following spring. So, the task for his men
was to lower a diversion gate, located at the mouth of
the flume, allowing the water to flow back to Humbug
Creek. Then, repair work could begin.

My clever uncle stole dynamite from the workers'
supplies, circled around them, and arrived upstream.
Tying dynamite to a large driftwood limb, he set the
log floating, playing out an attached line. When the
log and the explosives were in position, he lobbed a
stick of dynamite from a hill, and blew away the rock
wing dam. At this point, all the workers were stunned
and shocked by the explosion. Standing on a large
rock, my uncle addressed them, and said that such
actions would continue as long as Cort remained in

Yreka. Can you imagine his nerve and bravado? We later heard that the mine owner sold out and returned to the San Francisco area. Finally, Yreka was rid of Thorne Cort, that murdering scoundrel.

And that, my dear, is the last I know about Uncle Renke Vogel. In the period of two days, Cort's entire operation was ruined by that old man. Even though he was doomed to an early grave, there was a lot of grit in my uncle, wasn't there?

After kicking around in the Oregon mining camp, wanderlust took hold of me again. Lem had already left for the high life in St. Louis, and Gene had returned east to his relatives. While in Jacksonville, I made several friends, but none better than Doctor John Samuels. Surprisingly, he had tended my uncle when he practiced in Grants Pass. Jonah had already relocated to his farm on the Applegate River, and I visited him before traveling north. At the time, he was eyeing a girl who had traveled the Oregon Trail with her folks, and he later married her. (No, he never did look up that green-eyed gal in Grants Pass.)

As we parted, I had to hold back my tears as I hugged my brother for the last time. He was there for me whenever I needed him, and leaving truly wrenched my soul. He might have come with me, except his roots were already set in the land he was clearing. I have always missed him.

The long Willamette Valley in central Oregon led me to Oregon City, the end point for the trail of the same name. Along the way, wild berries, abundant at that time of year, kept me supplied, although the brambles were hell on earth, and sometimes I traveled a far piece just to skirt them.

I do vividly recall crossing the Columbia River, as it is surely as large as the Missouri, or maybe even the Mississippi. It was astounding, and I swore I would never cross it again until there is a bridge in place.

Ever northward, I rode my horse, until coming to the Nisqually River, which appeared to drain from the big, white-top mountain local folks called Tacoma. The mountain is surely as tall as Mount Shasta, yet rising more sharply. I ferried downriver with my horse to a large trading settlement founded and run by the Hudson's Bay Company. Beaver pelts were strung in long rows for curing. And many acres were planted, producing large stocks of food. I learned that this was a major port for the company, including the docks beyond the river delta, fronting the inland sea.

I decided to continue north in a dugout canoe, yet these boats were so highly prized that I could find no one who would sell. Not to be denied, I waited for the dark of the moon and stole one. There you have it! I confess to "borrowing" the dugout. Oh, I left a note with my compensation hanging from a nearby tree, and I also left my horse and saddle. I still think that it was a fair trade.

That night, I glided down the river, through the delta, and beyond the docks. As the moon rose, I turned the boat north. I later learned that I was paddling from the bottom of the inland sea and, generally, towards its ocean mouth, as the weather turned colder. Along the way, I also learned that it was much faster and easier to run with the outgoing tides than to fight the incoming flow. This left me with large stretches of time, as I waited for the receding tide. I fished and lived on the flesh of clams and oysters, which are in abundance along the shoreline. Have you ever tried these shell animals? Since that trip, the sight of them makes me ill. Yet, this food and my hardtack and berries kept me alive.

Weather conditions turned foul, with sheets of rain, then heavy fog. I had to take care not to be caught on the open water when the wind roared for fear of being swamped and drowned. In fact, the weather and fog were so heavy that I went straight beyond the largest town in the territory, Seattle, and two huge bays.

I became exhausted. The muscles along my ribs were strained from the hard work of paddling. I decided to go upriver at the next inlet, which turned out to be the Snohomish River, as I later learned. It was at flood stage, so I camped at its mouth for more than a week until water levels decreased.

The huge cedar trees lining the banks were inspiring and literally drew me up the river. I came to a farm owned by Mr. Cady, where I purchased powder and shot, as well as bacon and flour. I also made inquiries about inland areas. Following his directions, I continued up the Snohomish to its fork with the Skykomish River and took it northeast. Most of the names like "Skykomish" are Indian. This one means upstream people. I turned into still another waterway, called the Wallace River, and continued until I came to the gold mining camp at Gold Bar, which is located on the outskirts of an Indian village. Even though I had been told that the local natives were friendly, I turned downriver for about five miles and lighted on a likely place. I panned for gold and saw color, and that has become my land and home.

And that, dearest, is how I came to live along the banks of the Wallace River. Ever since, I have been alone, with no woman to take up my lodge. Yet, I have many friends, including Indian braves from the village I mentioned. Even so, all who shared my western journey have gone their different ways. My friend, Doctor John Samuels, has been a godsend to me. He has helped me get on with my life and, now that he has set up practice in Cadyville, I see him regularly. I can truthfully say that he has become like a brother to me.

So, dearest, know that you have a man here who loves you deeply and still has a hollow spot in him. That place in my heart is reserved for you. Come! Come fill it for me, and for us.

This letter is overly long, as I have dreaded coming to the end. I would be obliged if you indulged me this last thought.

My dearest, please understand that I cannot keep going on like this, waiting for your decision and living in doubt. Sorry to be blunt, my dear, but I need to have your answer. If it is no, then this shall be my last letter. I am not trying to pressure you. Either it is going to work for both of us, or we should get on with our lives.

Thank you for writing during these many months. It has been a wondrous experience for me. I pray your answer to marry me is yes, and that you will begin traveling west very soon, and that next Christmas, we will be together.

With all my love,

Frank

Additive: So you know all my flaws, I did attend schooling in Missouri, when farm chores permitted, but not often enough to write well, although I read constantly. My friend Doctor John has aided me. All the words and views in my letters are only from me. Of that, I swear and will do so on any family Bible you provide. The pen, however, belongs to my friend, John.

In the few moments that it took to read the last few lines, Eva's buoyant, happy mood swung to vexation at his ultimatum, only tempered by the warmth of his loving words. Swiftly, her feelings turned to righteous indignation, and her cheeks burned with humiliation. A stranger, at least to her, had read her letters, which expressed her private thoughts. Then, this doctor-friend had penned all of Frank's letters. And, her wild man had shared their personal exchanges right from the beginning, all because he could not write. She was stunned by these revelations.

Dropping her head, she sat as her tears flowed freely. Suddenly, she recalled poor Agnes, standing before the tribunal of women at the library association meeting. *My worst fear was that Frank was deceiving me with his letters. And Lordy, come to find out, he's another pen pal with buried truths.* Fiddling with her handkerchief, she suddenly straightened. *I know my next step. I have to talk with Viola right now.*

Hurrying to her sister's house, she went in, distressed and angry, as she fumbled in a pocket for her handkerchief.

Unsettled at the sight of a tearful Eva, Viola asked, "What are you crying about? Are these happy or sad tears that I see?"

Still clutching Frank's letter in one hand, she wailed, "Something terrible has happened."

Holding and petting her other hand, her sister asked, "Glory be, you've made your choice between Will and

Frank, haven't you? Tell me truthfully, have I guessed right? Yet, if that's the case, why are you crying?"

"It has nothing to do with Will. Frank let another man read my letters. Can you believe that? When I write to him, I express my feelings and hopes and dreams. The only other person who knows is you."

Gently, Viola pried the latest disaster out of her. When Eva finished telling about the ultimatum and a penman named John, her sister at first smiled; then, unable to contain herself, she broke away laughing. "Is that all there is to this calamity of stunning revelations?"

Taken aback by her sister's unflappable reaction, Eva heatedly replied, "Well, isn't that enough? He can't write, and on top of that, it seems perfectly obvious that a stranger has read every single word I sent, and written Frank's letters. Oh, Viola, I feel like I've been violated."

"My land, get a grip on yourself, sister dear. Haven't you been doing the same, when you share Frank's letter with me? Should he feel equally sullied?"

"It's different, because you're close kin and my best friend. Besides, I told him about you long ago in my letters."

Viola grabbed her shoulders and hugged her. "Girl, you have a man who worships the ground that you walk on. Yes, he's not fully literate, but you are, and you're a librarian. Heavens, writing can be learned, and you're exactly the right one to teach him."

"But this Dr. John Samuels, how do I know it's not his words that I've fallen in love with?" Suddenly, she stopped, stumped by hearing her true feeling spoken aloud. Then, she beamed. "Viola, did you hear what I just said? I'm in love, dear sister."

"Well, hallelujah! Now, at least two of us know the joyous news. Don't you think it's time you told that wild man in Washington?"

"Oh, yes," she replied, as all worries of dishonor vanished. "I'll write to him this very evening. I'm in love, Viola,

I'm in love, and I've made my choice," she sang, sashaying about the room and twirling in her full skirt and petticoats. Smiling broadly, Viola clapped and swayed, too. Eva continued her chant, in a singsong fashion—

> *"Frank be the choice, my wild man,*
> *so I'm leaving, to catch a train.*
> *Traveling to Washington, I am*
> *with the whole West, to tame.*
> *No one in the way, to stop me,*
> *I've finally made, my choice.*
> *It's off for my Frank, to see,*
> *to hear the love in my voice.*

It was barely rhythmic and far removed from the classical music they had heard when the symphony had played selections from Rossini and Paganini. Still, they laughed, did a do-si-do, and clapped—all at the same time.

"Indeed," Viola added, with zest, "you really have made your choice."

CHAPTER TWENTY-EIGHT

It was January, but the night sky was clear. Bundled in a fur coat for warmth, Eva looked at the sunset and commented, "What a beautiful evening. The air is crisp with a freshness you only get in winter."

Viola looked at her curiously, as they strolled toward their family home. "There's something different about you tonight, little sister, and I can't figure out what it is. I know you're in love and walking on a cloud, but something else is going on with you."

"I think you're right, there's lightness to my step these days. I feel wonderful and I'm excited about the trip, yet at peace. I received still another telegram from Frank."

"You did?" Her sister stopped, looking at her in amazement.

"He, or Dr. Samuels, had just read my response to his last letter. Do you want to know what he says in it?" she asked, coyly.

"Silly girl, read it to me. I've never known anyone who was courted by this modern telegraph system. Maybe someone will write a book about it."

Pulling the folded paper from her pocket, she smoothed it out and handed it to Viola.

THE WESTERN UNION TELEGRAPH COMPANY
——— INCORPORATED ———

Date	*January 22, 1889*
Rec.	*January 22, 1889*
Del.	January 23, 1889

Eva dearest. Marvelous news. I can't wait.

Send me telegram with schedule.

Please come soon. Love Frank.

"Oh, Viola, isn't it grand?"

"It truly is. When are you going to tell Father?"

"I'll confront the lion in his lair," she said with a laugh, "when I get in the house. I'll tell you tomorrow, how it goes." She opened the gate and waved good-bye before disappearing through the front door.

Viola lingered outside the fence. Reluctantly, she turned toward her home and whispered, "Ah, sister dear, you're fearless, and I love your spirit."

Eva entered the house and saw her father reading the newspaper in the sitting room. Primly, she sat in a straight-backed chair across the room from him, her hair up in a bun, as usual, and she smiled sweetly.

Her father put his paper aside. "Hello, my dear. You're looking very sprightly this evening, and you seem to have a glow on your cheeks. I'll bet you and Will have finally set the date for your marriage. Am I right?"

"Yes, I have."

"Well, by Jove, don't keep your poor, old father in the dark? When is it?"

"I am getting married next month, but not to Will."

"Eh? What in holy tarnation are you talking about, young lady?"

"I'm going to marry Frank Sommer, who lives in Washington Territory."

Isaac Helms stared at his daughter, confusion and astonishment vying for control of his face. He leaned forward in his easy chair. "Ah, well, ah, go on. Who in the world is this Frank . . . ah, what did you say his last name is?

"Sommer. I've been exchanging letters with him for more than a year. Months ago, he asked me to come west and marry him, and I've been thinking on it. Now, I've decided."

"Ye gads, woman, have you ever met this Sommer fellow? Or seen him in person?"

"I have a picture. Do you wish to see it?"

"When do *I* get to meet him?"

"You'll meet him when you and mother travel thousands of miles to the Northwest Territory. He lives outside the village of Snohomish, about twenty miles up the rivers. The largest town in the greater Puget Sound area is Seattle, which is fifty miles to the south. Frank owns part of a gold mine, built himself a new cabin, has land with vast timber interests, and fishes for salmon in the nearby rivers. He's originally from Missouri and ran off to go west when he was a lad. He's forty-eight years old now, and he's the man I love. I'm leaving on the stage a week from Saturday to begin my trip west."

Seeing the look on her father's face, she hurried on. "In Chicago, I board the Chicago and Northwestern Railway, which runs west to Council Bluffs, Iowa. There, I switch to the Union Pacific Railroad that runs to Ogden, Utah. And later, I take the Central Pacific to Sacramento, California."

"When do *I* get to ask a question about this . . ."

There was no stopping her, as she interrupted her father and continued. She relayed that a steamboat took train passengers downriver to the port of San Francisco, followed by a packet ship north to Seattle, and, lastly, the mail boat up the Snohomish River.

"Oh, my God," her father responded, exasperated. Leaning back hard in his chair, he had heard the gist of the travel details, but comprehension of the whole affair still lagged. Drawing himself up to stand and hitching up his pants, he asked, "Have you gone and lost your mind? Or, maybe you're just putting me on? That's it, isn't it, Ev? You're just jesting with your old father, because of the many times you and I have discussed this marriage business. I'm right, aren't I?"

Eva remained seated, in a ladylike manner. "No, I'm not funning you, and I've told you the way it is. And besides my future husband, you're the first to know my choice." She thought it best to make no mention of Viola. She watched patiently as his face drained, then returned to a mottled, reddish flush.

"How can you make such a rash decision? And, you've decided already and committed yourself? You made this choice without talking to me?" her father questioned. "And, you did this with no mention to your Mother?" Seemingly gathering himself, his questions and comments came in rapid succession. "Do you really mean that you're just going to up and leave us? And for what, some kind of flirty-thing, off in the deep woods with a man you've never laid eyes on? And right here in New Philadelphia, you'd turn away a fine upstanding man like Will, whom you've known forever. And you want to go to some untamed land, that's about as far removed from New Philadelphia as possible. Ev, you're really putting a big strain on your poor, old father's heart."

Eva remained silent and continued to sit primly. She was composed and strangely calm on the inside, while smiling sweetly, but mischievously, at her father.

"I won't stand for this lamebrain nonsense," Isaac Helms shouted. "I won't permit you to go! And, you can stop all this foolish talk right now. Do you hear me? I forbid it. The matter is closed."

"You forbid my marrying Frank?" Eva asked, dumbfounded. The hue of her face also raced toward red. "You won't stand for it?" she repeated, as she quickly stood, her head held high and her back straight as a rail. Her eyes nearly flashed with anger.

Wilting under her hard stare, Isaac Helms did the first thing that came to his mind; he tried to hide. Sitting down in his stuffed chair, he picked up the newspaper and opened it wide, separating himself from his daughter. It was a clever move, similar to the man closing the final curtain at the local theater. However, given his daughter's wrath, it was bound to fail.

Taking a deep breath to regain her composure, Eva said, "Dear Father, you can rant and rave until the skies fall in and the oceans rise. And you can try to vanish behind that newspaper, or even wiggle your ears in a cabbage patch, if you like. When it comes to my Frank and our plans, let me make it bell-like clear for you. Come a week from Saturday, I'm leaving on the stagecoach, and not you or anyone is going to stop me."

Fuming, her father crushed the newspaper in his lap. "Our Lord in heaven above, save this foolish woman. Eva, do you realize what you're saying?" he asked, his voice rising in alarm. "You're talking about going to *the* Wild West. You haven't forgotten the many stories about women being scalped, or worse, on the untamed frontier, have you? Good God above, it was only a dozen years ago that Crazy Horse caught General Custer dallying on the Little Bighorn River and dispatched him and his men, every last one of them." Pausing momentarily, he continued, "Maybe you've gone daft over this marriage business and temporarily lost your senses."

"No, you're wrong on that score. Father dear, you're the one who has reminded me for years that I'm a grown female, bordering on, if not beyond, spinsterhood. I'm a woman who is quite capable of thinking, feeling, and making my own choices."

"But Ev, this is so different from anything you've ever done or experienced before, how can you possibly know all the . . ."

Interrupting again, she continued, "You've lectured me day after day, month after month, for years to get on with my life, and now I'm doing exactly that. Short of the Almighty striking me down, I'm getting on that stage."

Beside himself, her father seemed to collapse into the back of his overstuffed chair and exclaimed, *"Good God Almighty!"*

"Yes, that's about right. The choice is mine, only mine. And my dearest, caring Father, I have made it."

CHAPTER TWENTY-NINE

With bated breath and trembling hands, Viola thanked the deliveryman, tore open the Western Union envelope, and read the telegram from her sister.

THE WESTERN UNION TELEGRAPH COMPANY
——— INCORPORATED ———

Date	March 11, 1889
Rec.	3/12/1889
Del.	March 14, 1889

VIOLA DEAREST STOP ARRIVED YESTERDAY STOP
I MADE GREAT CHOICE STOP MORE HANDSOME THAN
PICTURE STOP UNBELIEVABLE PANORAMA HERE STOP DETAILS
IN LETTER STOP REGARDS TO THE FAMILY STOP
EVA STOP

EPILOGUE

New Philadelphia

Viola returned home, carrying her groceries. At the mailbox, she scooped up the mail and hurried inside. Setting down her parcels, she quickly scanned the envelopes and dropped them when she came to one with a Washington Territory return address.

Fearing the worst about any revelations inside, she pulled out the letter. Calming herself, she began reading the letter from her sister.

March 25, 1889

To my closest friend and dearest sister,

My word, what an adventure I've had, crossing our big, wide country, traveling by train, at the lickety-split speed of over twenty-five miles an hour. Going downhill, it was even faster and nothing short of exhilarating. I don't know if you can imagine how swift that is. Why, standing on the train's rear platform, the rushing wind nearly left me breathless, as it tugged hard at my coat and skirts. I'm sorry, but the red hat you gave me as a parting gift is now somewhere in that wild country, swept off my head by an unexpected burst of wind.

Each evening, the train stopped at towns, and we stayed the night at hotels where we also took our meals. In Denver, at the foot of the Rocky Mountains, we stayed at the beautiful new Brown Palace Hotel. My word, it truly is an elegant wonder, with its open atrium lobby that is eight stories tall. Imagine standing in the middle of a building and being able to look straight up that high before seeing a ceiling. It was wondrous. I was told the hotel cost more than two million dollars to construct and furnish, and it's built of Colorado red granite and Arizona sandstone. Why, from the top-floor windows, I suppose folks can look straight out at the mountaintops.

The train climbed up and through the Rocky Mountains. It was more beautiful and inspiring than anything you can conjure up. We traveled on switchback rails and over bridges spanning broad, deep ravines. I saw many rivers and lakes, as we went through some of the wildest country to be had. When you come for a visit (remember, you promised), you will experience the same high adventure and sights, as I did.

I loved my stop in San Francisco. The city is built around a series of hills, overlooking a large bay on one side and the Pacific Ocean on the other. After leaving, I have to be honest, I was seasick during the entire ship passage north, as rough weather rolled us about, with waves breaking over the bow. I swear, the smoke from the twin stacks flowed back in straight lines that never varied unless the wind shifted.

Sailing into the Puget Sound, weather conditions cleared, and I saw headlands with the greenest and most abundant forests imaginable. Seattle is a thriving town, but it doesn't compare to San Francisco. It's also located on hills and seems rather helter-skelter, and I guess more typical of the frontier.

The packet boat trip north to Snohomish (they changed the name from Cadyville) was a joy, traveling under marvelously blue skies. I was excited, fearful, and panicked, all at the same time. Yet, there was no turning back at this point. My excitement built as the destination neared. I had sent Frank a telegram (wonder how they delivered it), letting him know my arrival date.

As the ship approached the dock, my heart sank. Among the large group meeting us, there was not one woman. Oh, how scruffy some of the men appeared. They looked and dressed rough, many with ragged beards and tattered hats. A few were outfitted in ragamuffin-like clothes. I swear, some had not seen soap and water for God knows how long.

My throat was dry, and I was having difficulty swallowing. I remember my legs felt unsteady, and my breathing became rapid. I felt a heavy weight in the pit of my breast, and my eyes were becoming teary.

As I desperately looked, searching the group for Frank, I held his picture in the palm of my hand. I studied each face on the dock. At that moment, my heart was beating wildly, and I was fast becoming panic-stricken, remembering all of Father's warnings. Then, I saw a tall man, standing over six feet. He stood out from the rest and came toward me, as I disembarked. He was broad of shoulders, just as we had guessed, and with the largest, kindest eyes that I have ever seen. It was my Frank. Oh, Viola, in an instant, I went from near hysteria to being wildly happy.

We awkwardly hugged, and he said he loved me and had longed for me all his life. His voice was soothing and deep, and I found myself calming down. Well, we wasted no time, as the minister was waiting for us at the hotel. A dozen of his friends attended, all neatly attired, and the ceremony was brief. He slipped a lovely gold band on my finger, and we kissed. Sister dearest, can you just imagine? Our first kiss, ever, came after I said 'I do.' I know you are smiling now.

The minister had us sign the marriage papers, and I did so for both Frank and me. Next, a dinner followed with his friends. Meeting Doctor John Samuel was a bit unnerving, but he was gracious, and my uneasiness passed. Then, we stole away to our room up the steps. I am blushing now! He was gentle, kind, caring, and all that I had ever longed for. The queen of circulating libraries, Mary Elizabeth Braddon, never wrote about the beautiful things Frank and I did on our first night. Good Lord, why didn't you tell me years ago?

Oh, Viola, I know this was the right decision. Even so, I will be haunted for the rest of my life by the memory of Mother standing on the porch, wringing her hands and crying out, 'Ev, please don't go.'

Anyway, before sunrise the next morning, we left for our home on the Wallace River. Fresh from a bountiful breakfast, we packed the supplies Frank had purchased the previous day, and my luggage, in his long, narrow canoe-like boat. It is hewed from a single log, split lengthwise, with most of the inside cut or scrapped out. Frank says it is safe and reliable, and he calls it a dugout.

He helped me into the bottom near the front, holding me steady as it rocked, and he bundled me in a warm beaver robe, then kissed me on the tip of my nose. Sitting in the stern, he paddled away from the dock. As we rounded a bend, the boat moved smoothly through swirling wisps of fog. Beyond, we broke out of the mist and sailed into our new life, with the rising sun brilliantly shining on the river before us.

Write soon, and start planning your journey.

All my endless love,
Eva

An aside ~ Say hello to the family for me. Tell father not to worry. His spinster-aged daughter is in capable and loving hands. However, you were right about my bustle. It travels very poorly on the frontier.

AUTHOR'S NOTES

It has been a pleasure to write the Six Bulls series of novels. The books contain accounts of pioneers who migrated westward in search of better lives, which resulted in the building of a nation. Their tales have been passed down through the generations. Combined with historical events, these provide a vast canvas for my novels.

As a youngster, my family moved west over the storied asphalt trail named U.S. Highway 66, the twentieth-century version of the dirt trails of previous centuries. Completed in 1938, the ribbon of road stretched twenty-four hundred miles from Chicago to Santa Monica, crossing eight states, and three-time zones. Known variously as "the Mother Road," "Main Street of America," and "Will Rogers Highway," it has been celebrated in many different forms. It was the route that breathed life into my boyhood dreams of adventures about pioneer trails, cowboys herding cattle, and Native Americans riding the open plains, created by books, movies, and magazines of the day. Decades later, my wife and I retraced this journey and more, in the current mode of the covered wagon, a motorhome, complete with several hundred horses.

From my research, it has been an honor to weave together an anthology of American westward expansion in the 1800s, from North Carolina, to Ohio and Indiana, southwest to Missouri, across the plains, through the Rocky Mountains, and finally to California, Oregon, and Washington. True enough, you'll not find the same interpretation in history books; nevertheless, it is my account of the western migration in the United States during the 1800s.

I marvel at the spirit of early pioneers who settled the American frontiers. They had perseverance, overcame many fears and self-doubts, and were, of necessity, self-reliant. They have my greatest admiration, and it is an honor to incorporate some of their experiences and family tales in all the novels, including this one. Here are a few instances ~

It was in Washington State that the woman behind the Eva character learned to fish, which became a lifelong hobby. Newly arrived from Ohio, she had some interesting, early encounters with local Native American women. This was particularly true the first time she was alone, while her husband went to town for supplies. Unannounced, some came to visit. Initially, she continued wearing clothes in an eastern fashion, including layered petticoats. As the women wandered into her cabin, she was frightened; then more so, when they insisted on seeing what lay beneath the outer skirt, by lifting one layer after another. Over time, she became fast friends with them and other pioneers who arrived in the thriving town that her husband helped establish. Her sister visited once, as did her former suitor.

The men behind the young brothers, Frank and Jonah, left their farm in southwest Missouri and traveled west, working on a wagon train, and, through a series of events, began ranching in the broad valley encompassing Yreka, California. Both men later left California and traveled north. The real Jonah settled on a quarter section of land in southern Oregon on the Applegate River.

His brother continued to Washington Territory. One family tale tells how the man 'borrowed' a dugout canoe from a trading post and paddled north, using the waters of the Puget Sound as his highway. Through the rain and fog, he missed seeing Seattle and continued to the Snohomish River, followed it up to the Wallace River, and settled there. He invested in gold mines, built a hotel, and, in mid-life, began exchanging letters with an eastern woman. This led to her traveling west and becoming his wife.

The 'Captain Renke Vogel' character in real life obtained his captaincy from fellow militiamen, who elected him an officer during the Black Hawk War. In other times, he farmed in Ohio. There are many tales about his size, strength, and love for boxing, taking on all comers. Joining other family members, he made the two-thousand-mile journey, using the big rivers of America, and traveled to the frontier in southwest Missouri and the lands called Six Bulls. At some point, he left Missouri, but later returned, seeking his final resting place. On a neighbor's farm, a fieldstone marks his grave.

I thank God for their adventurous lives
And the many memories bequeathed.
I pray that our nation continues to persevere,
And will always have a pioneering spirit,
Self-reliant and unafraid.

Buffalo Stampede

It may sound implausible for a man to confront stampeding buffalo and survive. Yet, such events are part of Rick Steber's book, *Tales of the Wild West, Volume 1*. He describes several encounters by settlers traveling the Oregon Trail, including a stampede that overran a man and his horse.

"Golden Showers"

There were many dangers on the westward trails in the 1800s, but trouble from Native Americans was not the greatest, despite the many novels and movies with that theme.

Some deaths on the trail were accidental. Pulling a rifle by the barrel-end out of a wagon bed was one of the more common. The sometimes-clumsy, heavily laden wagons weighed up to several thousand pounds. If anyone got in the way of rolling wheels, a limb could be crushed or a life lost.

All of these dangers paled, however, compared to the thousands who died from drinking polluted water. Some attempted to flee the dreaded illness by leaving their wagon train and joining another, only to have the sickness follow because of contaminated clothing and bedding.

Today, the disease is called cholera. For the most part, it doesn't infect cattle, but causes severe diarrhea in humans. It becomes deadly when the body becomes overly dehydrated. Additionally, the illness is easily transmitted. A solution of sugar and electrolytes is the international cure. Boiling drinking water would have saved the lives of many early pioneers traveling the western trails.

New Philadelphia, Ohio

The city is seventy miles south of Cleveland and one hundred-twenty miles northwest of Columbus. It continues to be the seat of Tuscarawas County. Initially established in 1772 as a mission to the Delaware Indians by the Moravian Church, it was founded by John Knisely. The man brought his family to the area in 1804, then hired a surveyor to lay out the town in a grid similar to it's namesake in Pennsylvania. In the 1880s, its population ranged between three and four thousand. Today, twelve thousand residents make it their home.

Sublette Cutoff

The Oregon Trail comes to a fork south of the Sandy River in Wyoming. Rather than continuing southwest to Fort Bridger, then doubling back northwest to Fort Hall, the Sublette Cutoff bisected the geographic triangle, saving some ninety miles and a week's travel time.

Blazed by mountain men Caleb Greenwood and Isaac Hitchcock in 1844, it became a favorite with gold miners. The trail was hazardous, as half of the journey went through semi-desert areas where water was scarce. West of the Green River, the trail crossed high ridges, some with an elevation of eight thousand feet. Despite the added dangers, the shortcut proved to be popular for those eager to shorten the distance to California or Oregon.

Cattle Drives

Spanish explorers and Catholic priests introduced cattle to the Western Hemisphere during their early explorations and settlements. According to folklore, cattle drives always went north and east from Texas and Oklahoma in the 1800s, not northwest. Were there actually cattle drives that crossed the Rocky Mountains, heading west? Yes, there are accounts found in several reports and diaries. Mayor James Sparks of Fort Worth, Arkansas was one man who led such a cattle drive (and, to my knowledge, he survived the journey).

The men who flocked to the west in search of gold had a vast appetite for beef. California ranchers supplied much of it. Additionally, cattle herds were driven south from Oregon farms and ranches.

Eastern-bred "Missouri beef" sold for a premium, despite the rangy-looking cattle. Some reports of the day say that a single animal sold for upwards of several hundred dollars, especially during the euphoric first days following a new gold discovery.

Yreka

In 1851, a heavy rainstorm pounded a group of prospective gold-seekers, as they traveled south from Oregon, through Northern California. One night, these men camped on the site that became known as "the richest square mile on earth." The next morning, the group's leader, Abraham Thompson, noticed the mules pulling up bunch grass. On the dangling roots, he noticed flecks of gold.

The mining town's initial name was Shasta Butte City, located on the banks of the creek running through the boomtown. The first tent structures were built on Main Street, today's Miner Street. In 1852, the town's name changed to Mt. Shasta-Yreka, and finally to Yreka. There are several stories connected to this unusual name. One is that it comes from a Native American word; another says that it is the reverse of the word "bakery" without the "b." Still another believes the name was originally misspelled.

Like many mining towns and camps, Yreka sustained several disastrous fires. The most significant one occurred in 1871. The central part of the town remains standing today, as durable brick construction replaced wood. Today, ranching, agriculture, and timber have replaced gold mining, and the population is about eleven hundred. It is a unique place, which is truly inspiring, set in a beautiful valley, surrounded by hills, mountains, rivers, and valleys.

"K"

The next novel will again be historical fiction, and it takes place in the farming hamlet of Am Furtt, situated at the toll crossing on the Kupi River, presently the border between Slovenia and Croatia. The story spans centuries, beginning with the vicious attacks over several hundred years by raiders from the Ottoman Empire followed by Napoleon's conquest in the early 1800s.

For half of a millennium, families in the serfdom called Kostel labored for absentee landowners. The serfs were tied to farmland, passing the right of use from father to son. Life was hard, and continued existence was difficult.

By the beginning of the 20th century, serfs were freed, and beautiful, dark-haired Katrina falls in love with an itinerant, handsome young Italian by the name of Leonardo. He's a happy-go-lucky sort, who loves to sing and tell stories, plays the trumpet, struts a bit, and is downright beguiling to beautiful Katarina. Their passionate love blossoms, only to be tested by hard times, the irresistible, siren call of a better life in America, and Katrina's wily grandmother—who is sternly old-school, wealthy, and the matriarch of a family living in the same village for four centuries—and her obstinate ways, "I demand your first child in payment."

"K" will be published in 2014 and is based on true events.

END

OTHER NOVELS AND SHORT STORIES

Novels Six Bulls Series ~

Six Bulls—The Ohioans (print and e-book versions)

Rafting from Ohio to Missouri down the big rivers of America, pioneers load their families and possessions on flatboats, seeking a new life on the American frontier. Adventures abound during their exciting and dangerous trip.

The Carolinian (print and e-book versions)

Abraham matures during the Battle of New Orleans and later applies those principles on his tobacco plantation in North Carolina. Shunning slavery, he moves his family west. Their adventures produce a riveting account of pioneer life in the wilds of a new country, while battling the ever-present Hooker, the slaver.

Avenge (e-book and print versions)

The theft of prized horses sets a young man on a journey of adventure. On the trail of the last outlaw, he roams the vast and wild American frontier, tracking the murdering rapist, as the two men clash in an epic battle of wits, where only one can survive.

Short Stories ~ These E-books are drawn from my novels.

Abraham

Abraham, the young raw-recruit, is exposed to the terror of war during the Battle of New Orleans. A frontiersman provides the wisdom to help him become a hero.

Arkansas Storm & Captain Jonathan Buzzard

Pioneers on flatboats are towed by a steamboat when they run into a storm that threatens their lives and the loss of all they own. In the next story, the big, brawny captain takes on the outlaws and saves the lives of his neighbors.

Beanblossom Creek & Stain

Chief Black Hawk's men are on the warpath, and the militia captain and his men are waiting. The battle that follows is tragic and larger-than-life. The second tale finds white settlers conflicted over the savage treatment of Indians.

Canyon of Death

The greatest killer on the Oregon Trail in the 1800s was unexpected, silent, and lethal. This pioneering party comes across a large herd of cattle and drovers that are dying. Read the story about *the* greatest killer on the California and Oregon trails.

Danny Boy and Tennie
Whimsical and humorous, a riverbank tavern on the Ohio River is the setting for pioneers quenching their thirst after their long wagon train journey to Indiana. It's a roaring good time, until a fight breaks out to enliven the evening. The second story is about Jonah and the green-eyed gal, Tennie, confronting a violent tornado storm.

Newtonia
Settlers on the frontier are caught between warring armies, as the Civil War rages. In the midst, human compassion is found.

Roaring River
Bushwhackers ambush two men, killing one. The survivor leads a posse to track down the band of killers, resulting in the battle of Roaring River.

Runaway Slave
A tobacco plantation owner is confronted with a split-second decision that will affect the rest of his life.

Smoke
Prairies are one of God's greatest gifts, but they can also be deadly. Rural pioneers take desperate measures, trying to save everything they have created on the wild frontier.

Sourdough Wind Mine
Deep in the bowels of the gold mine, the enforcer confronts men stealing gold.

Three Bells

Settlers on remote farms in Indian prepare to defend themselves against Chief Blackhawk and his warriors. One fateful night, an encounter changes everyone, forever.

Please visit my web site.
http://hstrial-rpuz.homestead.com/